1

FEAST OF FOOLS

AND OTHER TALES

Edited by R Poyton

www.innsmouthgold.com

THIS IS AN INNSMOUTH GOLD BOOK

ISBN 978-1-7391756-0-3

Copyright@ 2022 R Poyton.

www.innsmouthgold.com

Cover and interior art by
Shelley De Cruz
Copyright@2022 Graveheart Designs
www.facebook.com/graveheartdesigns

CONTENTS

FOREWORD

Corner me at sword point, and I'd say that my favourite literary genre is Sword and Sorcery. That's because as well as its own tropes, it can incorporate aspects of almost any other genre – action, cosmic horror, detective, adventure, noir, and so on. Take the most well-known S&S character, for example, Robert E Howard's Conan of Cimmeria. Across the twenty-odd original Conan yarns, we have mercenaries and pirates, police and thieves, kings and queens, fiends from the outer dark, frontier adventures, the undead, epic battles, grim humour, even a hint of romance.

Despite all this, S&S is usually derided, as a literary form. I can't help thinking that this is largely due to the slew of generic, mostly terrible, "barbarian "films that followed in the wake of 1982's *Conan the Barbarian.* While it was a sound S&S movie, that film, to me, was a poor attempt at depicting REH's Conan. I've written more on this in my book *Innsmouth Essays,* so I will say no more here! However, what the film did do, is set the standard for the barbarian movie. A huge, muscle-bound monosyllabic guy fights a monster and rescues the swooning buxom maiden. Our Hero is often accompanied by a comic-relief sidekick.

Yet even a cursory perusal of S&S literature reveals a range of styles and approach. Incidentally, I would highly recommend Brian Murphy's *Flame and Crimson* as an excellent and comprehensive history of the genre. So yes, we have the "founding figure" of Conan, though even that character, largely because of the movies and even worse TV series, has become reduced to a stereotype. REH's original is far more nuanced and has much more of a character arc than people might think. Outside of the Hyborian age, we have Leiber's Fafhrd and Grey Mouser, Karl Edward Wagner's Kane, Moorcock's Elric, C.L. Moore's Jirel of Joiry, Keith Taylor's Bard, Charles R. Saunders' Imaro and a host of others. All very different characters in very different settings, but all falling, at least in my view, under the S&S umbrella.

But what defines S&S, as opposed to fantasy? Opinions may vary, but most agree on a core set of principles. Fritz Leiber first coined the term, in response to a Michael Moorcock letter to the fanzine *Amra* in 1961. The latter had proposed the term "epic fantasy" to describe REH's work. Leiber replied, suggesting "sword-and-sorcery as a good popular catchphrase for the field." He expanded on this in the July 1961 issue of *Amra*:

"I feel more certain... that this field should be called the sword-and-sorcery story. This accurately describes the points of culture-level and supernatural element and also immediately distinguishes it from the cloak-and-sword (historical adventure) story, and from the cloak-and-dagger (international espionage) story too!"

The S&S tale, then, is generally characterised by a lone protagonist (as opposed to the "fellowships" of other fantasy works.) This individual is rarely, if ever, a "chosen one," or of noble birth. They are usually thieves, adventurers and the like. Not exactly clean-cut types, they are morally ambiguous, surviving by their wits and fighting skills. Many early S&S

writers, were influenced by the *Tales of the Arabian Nights*, and so usually feature some type of monster and/or evil sorcerer. Magic is a real thing, but is usually costly to the user - there are no teenage Wizard Colleges here!

Above all, S&S tales are fast paced, with an emphasis on the immediate situation over extensive histories or world-building. Characters are defined through their actions rather than lengthy internal or external monologues. Dangers, risks and rewards are immediate and personal rather than the world saving quests of epic fantasy. There may also be an argument that S&S should contain some element of cosmic or Lovecraftian horror. Such was certainly the case in the early days, perhaps no surprise given the close relationships between Lovecraft, Smith, Howard, Leiber, et al.

My own introduction to S&S began with books. As a young lad I devoured Tolkien's *The Hobbit* and Garner's *The Weirdstone of Brisingamen* alongside historical swashbucklers such as Dumas' *The Three Musketeers*. At the same time, we had those amazing films, such as *Jason and The Argonauts*. I'd defend to the hilt the opinion that Harryhausen's skeleton scene in that movie remains unrivalled as a piece of S&S cinema! Then, one day, my dad brought home a paperback - the 1973 Sphere *Conan the Adventurer*, with the iconic Frazetta cover, and a whole new world opened up...

And so, to this collection. In the past, Innsmouth Gold has focused primarily on the Lovecraftian, with a slight diversion into the King in Yellow mythos with our last release, *Corridors*. As such, I thought it was time to produce an S&S anthology.

Once again I called on the sublime talents of the Innsmouth Writing Circle and they did not disappoint! I'm also pleased to welcome some new authors to the Innsmouth fold – Gavin Chappell, Lyndon Perry, Ashely Dioses and HR Laurence.

What awaits within are tales of temple robbers, avenging warriors, lucky thieves, dealings with demons and missions to far flung places. Settings include cold, northern mountains, dreary swamps, Lovecraft's Dreamlands, dank dungeons, and mighty palaces. Furthermore, each story is prefaced with some wonderful artwork from our talented friends at Graveheart Designs. In addition, I'd like to thank all our supporters and backers, as ever, we couldn't do it without you.

All that remains then, dear reader, is to don your chain mail shirt, raise high your battleaxe, let loose a savage war cry, and plunge headfirst into a world of high adventure.....

Robert Poyton
October 2022

THE HORN OF TUR

- H R Laurence

"You worm," said the girl, scowling down at Heodric where he knelt, chained to the floor of the inner temple. "You shard of insignificance. You hopeless, thoughtless churl - how dare you try to steal from this most holy of places?"

She paused as the High Priest spoke again, his voice booming in the great vaulted chamber. Few beyond the sacred island could comprehend the ancient ritual language of the Priests of Tur, and the girl's pretty face wrinkled with concentration as she listened. For a charming moment she bit her lip, considering how best to translate the archaic tongue. Then she turned back to Heodric, and her scowl returned.

"You blasphemous ape," she said. "You barbaric unbeliever. You troglodyte."

Heodric's head was throbbing from the beating he'd received, and he didn't have much idea what a troglodyte was. He had more important things to dwell on in what might be his final moments, and so as the girl continued, pausing regularly to receive and translate fresh insults from the Priest, he let her words wash over him and considered these things in the order that they occurred to him.

First, the chains which bound him. They were too strong to break. Second, the half-a-dozen temple guards about him, each a veteran fighting man with the scars to prove it. They were too many to fight unarmed. Third, the wide windows of the chamber - tempting, eminently jumpable. But - fourth - the long, sheer plunge onto jagged rock beneath them, and - fifth - the many miles of rough sea to swim should he survive it. The obvious conclusion was a grim one. He decided to listen again, and see if there was any comfort to be heard.

"...so doubt not that you will die here, thief," the girl was saying. Heodric gave the smallest of sighs. He didn't doubt her at all, and so he decided to make his peace with what approached. Young though he was, he knew Death well. He had faced Her in the ranks of the shield-wall, fighting as an auxiliary for the Zyrenian Emperor; and on the tossing deck of a trireme, fighting as a mercenary for the Emperor's Kretan rivals. He had faced Her in dark alleyways and taverns, dirk in hand as he fought for merchant princes and crimelords, and he faced Her now - about nobody's business but his own.

He was glad of that, though he did wish that he had thought his business through a little more carefully. The sacred isle of the bull-god Tur had been a tempting target, for Tur was revered by the fighting-men of Zyrenia and its colonies, and in consequence His temple dripped with golden plunder. Heodric had imagined it would be simple to blend in amongst the many pious military pilgrims, but the Priests of Tur were canny as well as strong, and some small slip - an ill concealed smirk, a rogue twinkle in his eye - had betrayed his lack of sincerity. When the guards found lock-picks on his person his fate was sealed.

And so he knelt in chains upon the grated and bloodstained floor where young bulls were sacrificed every morning in Tur's honour, with the tiered dais before him rising like a ziggurat to nearly twice his six feet in height. The translating slave-girl sat on the upper steps, and above her the High Priest slouched in a great chair of ivory, its arms curved and pointed like the horns of a huge bull. He was a tall man, though age and indulgence had lessened what must have been a mighty frame - the skin of his arms was loose where there had once been hard thews, and beneath a golden breastplate filigreed with rippling muscle there was a bulging, well-fed belly. The right side of his face was a pulpy mass of old scar, with a hollow socket - for Tur's priests needs must have bled in his service - but at his left hand was a platter of grapes and sweetmeats, and a flagon of wine.

Heodric saw no wisdom or mystery when he looked upon the High Priest; just an old officer gone to seed, invalided out of the army and in need of a new profession where he could spend his days giving orders. It was hard to stand condemned by such a man; harder still to respect his sentence.

He lowered his gaze to the Temple Guards before him, and they glared back at him with undisguised hostility. They were fighting men like he; he had imagined they might understand one another. But he saw no understanding in their furious gaze. The Temple Guard was itself the lowest rank of the Priesthood, made up of veteran soldiers who had pledged themselves to the service of Tur. Each man of them yearned to someday be atop the dais with the High Priests - to learn the mysteries of Tur and eventually put aside his blade and take relish in the luxuries won not by their own strength but that of their god. Heodric felt no fellowship with such men; it would be hard to die at their hands.

He lifted his eyes again, this time to the High Priest's slave. She glared as fiercely as the men, but she was far more pleasant to look upon - no surprise, since Tur's portion of plunder included the choicest captives. She sat with her long legs stretched out, auburn hair tumbling over her bare shoulder, golden baubles glimmering at her slim throat - and as she proclaimed the next tranche of insults, Heodric thought he detected something of an actress' relish in the way she spoke, as though she was secretly amused by the absurdity of the abuse she heaped upon him. He found it hard to believe that she really thought he was a worm.   In fact, he found himself wondering whether she might not have rather liked him, had they met in happier circumstances. Before he could continue that thought any further, the High Priest outstretched an arm, and spoke with an air of finality.

"You shall be thrown into the Horn of Tur, and at its tip devoured by the avatar of the god," the slave-girl said. "Pray that he accepts your death as sufficient punishment, and does not flay your soul perpetually in the eighteenth hell."

Heodric realised that while trying to make his peace with Death he had struck inconveniently upon a strong desire to stay alive - if only to spite the Priest's sentence, thwart the guards, and become better-acquainted with the slave-girl. He flexed his arms against the chains, but they had become no weaker in the few minutes since he last tested them. The guards stepped forward, and he tensed. They would have to loosen his shackles to take him, and the moment they did...

A spear-butt struck his head and sent him sprawling. As the world came back into focus the guards swiftly removed his chains, and as he began to thrash, wordlessly lifted him, a man to each limb. Metal screeched; Heodric twisted in his captors' grasp to see that the grated floor was sliding away, revealing a huge opening. The sides of the pit gleamed; they were of polished bronze and they sloped and curved inwards like an inverted cone, narrowing to a point where a jagged hole gaped. It was as if he was at the rim of a giant drinking-horn. For the first time he felt real horror, for this was a foul, undignified end - to be thrown away like an unwanted scrap. And even as he mustered his strength to fight back, they swung him back and flung him into the pit.

For a moment he felt himself hang in air, and then he was falling. He slammed against the smooth metal of the horn and went tumbling, sliding in a wide, rapid spiral down the narrowing wall. His boots scraped uselessly; his fingers scrabbled at the bright sheet-metal. There were channels in the side of the horn for the blood of sacrificed bulls to course down, too tiny to grip, but chiseled sharply enough to score his groping fingers. Round he went, tumbling head over heels. The dark hole came looming up, and more through luck than design he lashed out with a leg and caught the opposite side of the horn, instinctively straightening to brace against the sides with his arms and legs outstretched. He slid to a halt, only feet above the gap. The aperture was near as wide as he was tall: he was only just able to wedge himself above it. Within moments his taut body was burning with the strain.

A guardsman's face appeared at the top of the pit, and frowned to see him. A word of command was spoken; he heard the whirr of a pulley, the groan of a counterweight. Hatches opened in the sides of the horn above him, so cunningly designed that he would never have guessed they were there. Seawater rushed out and came coursing down the sides of horn. The torrent struck him hard; he slipped a little, and then felt his hands sliding against the wet metal. For a desperate moment he struggled - and then more water fell and the flood bore him down.

With a cry he caught at the rim of the hole and swung there, the whole weight of his broad body held by his fingertips. Pain lanced through his hands and forearms. Gazing into the black pit below he sought for safe place to fall - but he could see nothing. Water surged past him; filling his eyes and ears, drenching his head. He heard it spatter faintly against rock below - and then a deeper splash as some stray droplets struck the surface of a pool.

From above he heard the groan of the pulley once again; he couldn't hold here against another deluge. As the dregs of the first torrent trickled past him he listened desperately for the sound it made. There it was. The faint chime of water on water, somewhere to his left - and deep below him. It was a tiny chance, but he had to take it. Arms burning, hands afire, he swung himself once, twice, and with the last of his strength launched himself into the dark.

He struck it feet first. Then the world was black and freezing, rushing all about him, filling his eyes and ears and throat. Heodric felt himself sinking, and as he stretched out to swim his elbows struck with jarring, scraping pain against rock. For a brief moment he was a lost and frightened animal, somehow crammed into a space so narrow that it was impossible to swim. How could it be that the void into which he had fallen was suddenly so tiny? Every instinct screamed at him to swim and gain the surface - but his lashing out earned him nothing but bruises against the hard walls of his watery prison. He was blind, and the shock of cold was fast giving way to pain. The breath was all but gone from his lungs. Somehow he fought against the panic that threatened him. He twisted, bringing his right arm above his head. His fingers brushed against a join in the stone. He held himself in place, and found purchase on the rock with his feet. Lungs bursting, he clambered up the rocky shaft until he broke the surface of the water.

Heodric gasped. He was at the centre of a shallow rock pool, with the dark shaft into which he'd fallen at its centre. A cold shiver went through him as he realised how extraordinarily lucky he had been: a foot to either side and he would have struck the bottom of the pool and shattered there. Shards of bone and rag on the rock testified that he wouldn't have been the first.

Heodric rose, soaked and shivering. He was in a wide, rocky cavern, though patches of worked stone showed where passageways had been cut or enlarged by the Priests. The crevice into which he had first fallen must have been a drainage shaft, for he could hear the roar of the sea close at hand. The light from the horn above was lessening as the grate slid back into place, and the last thing he noticed was that the nearby bones were not just broken, but chewed. He waited long moments for his eyes to adjust to the gloom, shivering in the cold. It was possible, he thought, that there were stray dogs in these caves, but not terribly likely. Heodric's ears were keen, and over the roar of the sea and his own ragged breath he was soon aware of a heavy approaching tread...

The girl had said he would be eaten by the avatar of Tur. Insofar as Heodric had thought about it, he had assumed that the devouring was to be a metaphorical one - but the thing that was now approaching didn't seem to be much of a metaphor. With his slow-returning sight he could make out a large shadow at the edge of the cavern, emerging from one of the many branching caves and corridors. As it straightened he caught his breath. It was near twice his size, and Heodric was a big man. It had a broad bull-like head and great half-curved horns as long as Heodric's arms; but the trunk of the beast was like that of a great ape, shuffling half-upright upon the knuckles of huge hands. It paused and sniffed, nostrils like gaping cave-mouths snuffling in the cold air. Then the great head lowered, and red eyes narrowed. It was looking straight at him.

Fear lanced anew through Heodric's frame, but he didn't move an inch from where he crouched. After a long moment the beast's head turned, scanning from side to side. It had his scent, but it saw no better in the gloom than he did. And as it began to approach, huge and dark, Heodric saw that it was slow, its progress painful, its huge legs near-hobbled with arthritis. The avatar of the god was old. It must have been many years since it encountered any prey which had not first been crippled upon the rocks, since no predator in such condition would survive long.

And yet its thews were vast, and its horns long, and the teeth that its thick and slavering lips now drew back from were sharp enough, if perhaps fewer than they had once been. In a contest of brute strength it might still master him. It was close now, and he could smell its odour - rank and musty, a damp animal stench. Perhaps sensing that he was near, it gave a low growl of challenge and scanned the rocks anew - and this time when the huge red eyes alighted upon him they did not pass, but widened a moment in greedy recognition. Heodric tensed. It shuffled a step towards him, and hesitated - for it could see now that Heodric lived, and yet did not whimper or moan like the wounded morsels it was accustomed to. Somewhere in the great bull-skull was a faint memory of strong prey which had fought back, and fought hard before being killed.

Heodric sprang before it could resolve itself. His legs snapped straight; the huge form flinched before him - and he sailed over its head, and landed lightly behind it. It whipped about - too slow - and the beast grunted surprise and then roared alarm as his brawny arm went about its thick corded neck. Heodric felt himself lifted clean from the floor, and clung grimly on. But its neck was huge and thick, and pulsing with muscle. He strove in vain to crush the breath from it, and the monster moved beneath him, bearing him painfully towards the sharp rocks where he had crouched. He realised its purpose, and as it rolled to crush him he released his grip and caught hold of its vast horns, hauling himself across and above the great head so that the whole of his weight was atop it when it went down.

It crunched against the rocks with a horrible, fleshy impact, and the noise of its roar struck him almost as hard as the lashing of its body. It bellowed pain, and its teeth gnashed, and its huge head tossed. As Heodric rose a sharp horn came rushing towards him, scoring the air. He caught hold of it, and as the beast tried to toss him away he braced his foot against its huge skull, and wrenched. Sinew tore and cartilage buckled, and the avatar of Tur howled as Heodric tore its horn away. It tried to rise, with no thought now but to escape, and as it came to all fours the barbarian brought the huge horn down point first.

The bellowing ceased. Heodric drew a long breath, and then another, and looked down at the great body. In death it seemed suddenly pitiful. Whether natural-born beast or sorcerous chimera, it hadn't led much of a life - imprisoned in dank, cold caverns, awaiting the human scraps flung to it by the priests. Well. Perhaps it had gone to a happier time in one of the many hells of Tur, where it could gorge itself eternally on the flesh of the damned and the fires were always hot. Heodric turned from its corpse, and grinned to himself; what now, Priests of Tur? What now?

He found the passageway from which the beast had first emerged, and followed it. Chewed bones, and scratched rocks; a pitiful nest of torn hide and fabric in a crevice. The rock passage grew dark, but Heodric made his way along it until he saw a flicker of light ahead, glinting from a gate of polished steel. It was locked, and battered where the beast had flung itself against the bars. Heodric smiled without humour; the Priests had apparently not cared that the avatar of their god sought to escape them. Surely that was a sort of blasphemy. No matter - the beast had possessed no guile beyond its strength, and the lock was simple. He picked it with a shard of bone, and went into the corridors beyond.

Soon enough cave-rock gave way to paved stone, and he passed through cellars piled high with all manner of debris. Long-burning radium braziers hung from the ceiling, casting flickering red shadows from crumbling statues, taken from the frontage of the temple and weathered by the harsh sea air into weird, misshapen golems.

Clearly these deep passageways had become a repository for every object for which the priests had no use but did not care to destroy; he passed piles of empty amphorae, heaps of mildewed military cloaks, rusting heaps of swords dedicated to the god. He rooted through one of these, and found a blade less decayed than the others. The weight in his hand was a comfort. Large cavernous storerooms branched off at regular intervals, and from time to time he peered into them. In one room there were a hundred idols, dragged from the temples of conquered peoples, flung in tribute at the feet of Tur, then dumped in an ignominious cellar beneath them. In another, he discovered a dozen mummified corpses with bull horns sewn to their desiccated skulls: victims of some hideous ritual. In a third, the bones of sacrificed cattle had been fashioned into a cage and placed atop a pyre of dry wood, but for some reason lost to time never ignited.

From a long distance behind him there came a cry of alarm. Heodric glanced back. It was hard to tell, but he thought it must come from the cave at the bottom of the horn. The Priests had discovered the body of their pet.

They would have an easy time finding him if he lingered here, for the corridor had not branched off once. He hurried on. The path forked ahead, and he took the turning that seemed darkest. A short flight of stairs brought him to a large chamber, lined with glass jars as large as he was, copper pipes coiling all about them and stretching to the gloomy ceiling. They glowed softly, full of a murky, greenish liquid in which indistinct forms floated. He went uneasily between them. He could not quite see what was within the huge jars, and the shadows between them were long, for there was no light in the room save the glow of the freakish liquid. Ahead, red radium light illuminated the arch of a stairwell. He was almost upon it when he heard footsteps, and dove at once into the shadowy corner of the room.

Two guards had entered from the way he came, torches

flickering in their hands and casting orange glints from the sharp heads of their spears. They had caught up with him quickly, he thought, gripping his sword tight. The leading man muttered a word to his fellow, and they parted to sweep the shadows. Heodric tightened his grip upon his sword. He was in luck, for these men were over-confident and thought him unarmed. They would not have long to regret their error.

As silent as a cat, he slipped between the jars, flitting from shadow to shadow. Soon he was close to the first guard, coming up behind him as the man squinted oblivious beneath his torch. He brought up the sword, and his design fell apart. Wires were strung between the great vats, thin and imperceptible as spiderwebs. The sword scraped against them. It was only the faintest of sounds, but it was enough. The guard spun about with a cry. Heodric struck at him, but the man was swift and caught the blow on the shaft of his spear. He sprang back, his darting lance seeking Heodric's heart. The barbarian parried, but with a deft flick of his wrists the spearman brought his weapon about to strike at him again.

The guardsman knew his business; he drove Heodric back with swift, precise jabs, never overextending his weapon or giving the barbarian a chance to rush beyond his guard. The head of his weapon was long and serrated, and any opponent seeking to grab the shaft would like-as-not lose their fingers.

"Tyrus!" the man shouted. Footsteps echoed as the second guardsman came rushing to his aid. In another moment, Heodric would be facing them both at once. He didn't care to do that, and so he fell stumbling back. The spearman drove on at him, and Heodric retreated until he felt the glass of the nearest jar at his back. He had just had time to register that it was uncomfortably warm before the spearman drove at him. Heodric leapt aside; the spear struck home and with a crunch of glass it penetrated the jar and stuck there. For a moment the guardsman stood horrified as cracks shot across the surface of the vessel. Then it burst, and a torrent of green ichor flooded out atop him. The man screamed. The liquid hissed as it struck him, burning through spear and armour and skin alike.

Heodric rolled to avoid the flood, and as he caught his breath he gasped. The stuff smelt like the tomb; a musty, sharp stench which stung at his eyes and nostrils. The coppery smell of blood mingled with it now. In the centre of a smoking puddle before him, the melting corpse of the guard twitched its last. His late-arriving comrade Tyrus stood open-mouthed and horrified, and then his eyes lit on Heodric.

Heodric leapt, clearing the smoking mess between them. Tyrus parried his blow and rapidly span the spear like a quarterstaff to block the next thrust. Heodric feinted, and drove low, almost catching the man off guard. Tyrus skipped back just in time, and Heodric's sword struck the cobbled floor and broke there. He sprawled after it. A fine gift to Tur that was, he thought, and rolled to avoid a spear thrust. No wonder they left it in the cellar. The spear lanced down again; he twisted out of its path and caught the shaft above the serrated head before Tyrus could pull it up. With a yank he brought the man down atop him. Now they were wrestling together across the spearshaft, spitting muffled curses as they fought with their knees and elbows, neither wishing to relinquish his grip upon the weapon.

They rolled, forward and back. Tyrus was nearly as tall as Heodric and as broad, and his back was protected from the cobbles by his armour. He had soon gained the upper hand, and

Heodric felt himself dragged slowly and inexorably across the rough floor. A cruel gleam shone in the guardsman's eyes. Heodric felt heat upon his face: Tyrus meant to plunge him into the acidic puddle which still hissed and steamed on the floor. He kicked and struck, his blows bouncing futilely from the guardsman's armoured form. Another moment and he would be burned. *To hell with it.*

He let go of the spear and plunged his hand into the green liquid, ignoring the scorching agony which abruptly lanced through him. His fingers closed about a fragment of shattered glass; he drove it up and Tyrus gurgled for a moment as it found his throat. Then he keeled over, and Heodric came up gasping in pain, wiping his hand free of the burning liquid.

The first guardsman's fallen torch still burned faintly on the floor. Heodric picked it up in his good hand, wincing a little. The burn was a bad one; he would not be wielding a sword for some days. As he turned away his eyes lighted upon a small still shape lying on the cobblestones. Something else had come out of the jar. Heodric's curiosity bettered him, and he peered. What he saw made him curse with disgust. It was the body of a half-grown child, fused to the misshapen head of a calf, and with its sickly scrawny torso punctured with the copper tubes which had twined about the vat. There was no doubt now that what he had killed was something grown here - though he had neither seen nor heard tell of such diabolical sorcery before.

With a shudder he left the abomination, and went up the stairway. It brought him to another wide chamber, this one lined with high pillars beneath a vaulted ceiling. It was the main storeroom of the temple, set with dozens of arched doorways. Narrow stairwells spiraled up beyond them to the many sub-alters and chapels of the temple. Before him stretched an avenue of bronze tripods, silken alter cloths, and amphorae full of the sacred, scented oil with which the Priests anointed themselves. At the far end was a single stairwell, larger than the others, and at the foot of it stood a dozen temple guards with gleaming shields. They grinned in triumph and relief, for there was no contest here. The lone intruder was outnumbered a dozen-to-one, and bore nothing but a torch.

"Yield," said their leader. "Before you face the consequence of yet more blasphemies."

Heodric considered this. Then he smiled. "I"ve already killed a god," he said. "I can hardly do worse than that."

Their faces clouded and they started forward. Heodric stepped back, and with a single thrust of his broad arm he tipped the nearest amphora into their path; it shattered, and a wave of scented oil swept across the floor. They looked down as it soaked their sandaled feet, and back up as Heodric hefted the torch in his hand and raised an eyebrow. There was a clatter of falling spears, a splash of feet in thick liquid, and then a dozen men were fleeing back up the stairs as fast as their oily feet could carry them. Heodric tossed the torch after them and sprinted in the other direction. He felt a warm gust at his back as the oil ignited, heard the yelps of the fleeing guardsmen as he went tearing up the nearest staircase. He ignored the first few doorways off, for height was what he wanted now. Only when he saw daylight through an arrow-slit window did he pause.

The sea sparkled blue in the distance, and the long russet-tiled roof of the main temple complex stretched before him. Heodric saw with some consternation that thick smoke was rising from a corner of the building, and there seemed to be consternation in the crowds on the plaza before it. His fire had spread rather further than he had imagined. Well, it would keep his pursuers busy.

On he went, up the spiraling stairs, and through the first door he came across. Half-mended altar cloths hung on deserted looms, and a broad window afforded him a good view of the rear of the temple complex, nestling amongst the rocky heights of the island. A smile spread across his face. Beneath the window was the roof of an annexe, only a short drop, and mere feet from the far end of it rose the Red Tower, the dwelling place of the High Priest of Tur. It was very pretty in the evening sun, and he made a note to admire it, once he was far enough away.

With his burned hand, the exterior of the tower would be a challenging climb, so he simply dropped to the ground from the roof of annexe, and walked through the open door of the tower. There were no guards in sight. Someone had smiled on him this day - perhaps even Tur himself, delighted to see at last a little war brought to his placid domain. Heodric flexed the fingers of his good hand as he ascended the spiral staircase. He would be happy to see the High Priest again. The tower was tall, and his breath was starting to come short when he rounded another spiral and saw golden trappings and hangings of red silk, and a dull iron portcullis which barred his way into the rich chamber beyond. A door opposite led to a second stairway, and in the middle of the room the tall High Priest lay across a tousled couch with his throat cut, a look of surprise still faintly apparent in his one eye. The translating slave-girl bent across his body, a knife in her hand and her slim arm bloody up to the elbow. She was removing the jewels from his golden breastplate.

Heodric pushed against the portcullis. It was firmly locked, and the mechanism was well-crafted: without his picks it might take him hours to break. The girl looked up at him. She was playing a part no longer; there was real fury in her green eyes.

"You wretch," she hissed. "A whole year it took to get here - to have myself sold to the priests' service, and learn their rotten tongue, and gain their confidence. I've learned passwords - stolen keys. Another month, and I'd have cleared out half the whole treasury."

A shout came from somewhere below; a distant clatter of arms. She spat. "No chance of that now that you've set it on fire," she said, and ripped the Priest's golden necklace from his torn throat. A satchel lay open on the bed, and jewels and coin gleamed within it. "Now I've nothing but these baubles!"

It seemed to Heodric that she carried a small fortune. "I'm sorry to have upset your plan," he said, mildly. "But perhaps you might take me to the treasury anyway? You seem a resourceful girl. I'm sure the two of us might make a fair go of it."

She looked him up and down. Perhaps she liked what she saw, for the corner of her mouth twitched into half of a smile. "There's a boat beneath the north tower," she said. "But it won't linger long. You'll have to make your way through the temple."

"Let me come with you," said Heodric.

She shook her head, and now her smirk was unmistakable. "No," she said. "I think not."

She tossed the dagger to him between the bars, and as Heodric caught it left-handed he heard men calling from below. The girl winked.

"Good luck!" she said, and disappeared into the doorway beyond.

Heodric sighed, and hefted the dagger, slick with the cooling blood of the High Priest. Down the stairs, and then through the burning temple, and out into the cloister-maze beneath the North Tower - and all of it with one good hand. "Good luck" indeed. He would need it.

Then he smiled, for he had a weapon, and his strength, and had slain priest and demon and guardsman alike. A boat beneath the north tower? *Very well.* He would rise to the challenge.

"Tur," he said, as footsteps echoed in the stairwell. "Watch me."

TO TAME A DEMON

- Lyndon Perry

From the bottom of a dark pit, the rubied demon gazed up at its captor and his companion, eyes blazing gold and scales shimmering blood red. Two translucent wings fluttered in determined, dangerous rhythms. Master Fraughten, the ancient Citadel's demon keeper, tossed the devilish creature a large beef shank while his guest looked on.

"Fine specimen you have there," sniffed Master Oralon. "An incubus, I see. Or something quite close."

"Actually, it's an azaribub, a cousin to the incubus, although there's some debate as to their exact relationship," the demon keeper responded.

"Ah yes, I've heard of these creatures. Believed to be near the bottom of the hierarchy, akin to the imp, since they likely lack intelligence and moral reasoning."

Below them, the azaribub grunted, grabbed the bone, and began to gnaw on it. Lifting its head, it seemed to debone the two men with its raging eyes. Oralon heaved his impressive bulk to the railing to get a better look. The demon spat fire at the fat magician, and the impudent guest jerked back in alarm.

"I think it disagrees with your assessment," said Master Fraughten, chuckling.

The two sorcerers watched as the demon flexed its aquiline frame and stood to its full seven feet in height. It threw the shank aside and began to climb the moss covered wall of the deep, dank pit. Wisps of flame and smoke emanated from its nostrils.

Master Oralon brushed at his robe nervously. The slight blur of the magic barrier atop the cistern should have assured him he was safe. The demon could never reach them. Nevertheless, he gave the Hell-spawn's deep cell a wide berth as he moved for the exit.

"Quite...enlightening," he said.

"Quite," agreed Master Fraughten, turning from the demon and its pit.

The wizards walked slowly up the stairs, leaving the castle's lower levels and the putrid smell of the dungeons behind. Fraughten explained the process of summoning the azaribub as they climbed their way up to the main keep.

"I'll let you in on a little secret, my friend," the diabolist said. "We had no idea what the spell would conjure, quite frankly. The grimoire was quite faded. We were expecting a simple imp, in all truth." He opened his hands in a what-can-you-do gesture.

The visiting thaumaturge pulled up short. "Isn't that a dangerous exercise, Master Fraughten? I would think you and your colleagues here at the Citadel would take every precaution when researching a spell. One should never cast if the results are not guaranteed."

Fraughten merely shrugged as he reached the top of the stairwell, outpacing the overweight mage by a dozen steps.

Oralon persisted. "Weren't you concerned you might

summon a beelzebul or even one of the djinn?" The sorcerer made to catch up to his host, huffing heavily.

"Quite impossible, let me assure you, given the limited inherent power of the theurgical object we had available."

Fraughten turned and smiled blandly at his fellow Master. At the top of the stairs, the demon keeper opened the great oaken doors. Oralon, heavy laden by years of fine feasting, finally made it to the dungeon's exit.

"But of course, a pastime such as this always carries a certain element of risk, eh, Oralon?" The younger, thinner sorcerer laughed, dismissing the matter with a wave of his hand.

The Master flinched at such familiar address. Evidently, breaking protocol was a habitual pattern for his host, as well as the brotherhood here at the Citadel. He harrumphed.

They left the lower keep. Master Fraughten closed and locked the double doors, depositing a burnished key into an inner pocket of his dark and flowing velvet robe.

"Rest assured, *Master* Oralon" the younger mage said, picking up on the elder magician's objection to his informality, "we adhere to the strictest of safety measures. They just happen to be slightly different than those suggested by our beloved Masters' Great Council." Fraughten smiled at his companion once more, this time with a hint of malice.

"Yes, yes, I'm sure," Oralon nodded sagely, his jowls shaking. Sweat glistened on his high forehead and balding pate. "Tell me this, though, if I may be so bold."

Fraughten pointed the way to a door that opened into his private study, a cozy den with walls of shelves overflowing with manuscripts, scrolls, tomes, and quartos. The two men entered to a small fire burning in the fireplace, cutting the chill. The pleasant aroma of books, wood smoke, and herbs filled the air. The host motioned for the elder mage to be seated in a plush chair facing the hearth. The younger man took the chair opposite. A small table separated them; a silver tray boasted a decanter of port and two crystal dessert wine sippers. Master Fraughten poured each of them a generous glass and said at last, "Of course, Master Oralon. Please, be bold."

"What is the most powerful demon you've summoned so far?" The guest cleared his throat. "There is talk among the other fellowships that you actually *did* invoke a djinni, but did not have the power to control him." Oralon tasted the port, nodded in satisfaction, then took a healthy swallow. "Is there any truth to this rumour?"

"What have you heard, specifically?"

The visiting Master sighed. "Surely, you cannot deny the evidence of demonic activity in the area. Manor Hunesthall reported the disappearance of a young initiate just last week, believed to have been taken by an untethered devil."

"I'm well aware of the unfortunate occurrence at Manor Hunesthall. Tragic, indeed. But as to the demon's exact nature, I understand that has not yet been determined. It was just as likely a wild-roaming incubus. Not all of them have been recaptured since the disaster at Garin's Hall."

"I'll grant the possibility. Nevertheless, the recent spate of supernatural events has the Great Council worried, very worried indeed. They voted to prohibit the Seven Manors from summoning any new demons, you know. Your azaribub specimen is the last to have been called from Hades. And of course, they will not allow any Master to untether any devil in their holds."

"Nor should they."

Oralon set down his glass in surprise. "But Master Fraughten, it is well known that you and your colleagues at the Citadel have requested permission to expand your research and experiment with summoning higher level demons, including the highest order of djinn."

"That is correct. But we have not received such permission, nor have we any desire to unleash an untethered specimen. It would be the height of irresponsibility."

An uncomfortable silence filled the gap between them, broken only by the crackling of the fire in the hearth. The visiting wizard took another sip of port.

"Let me be blunt," Oralon tried again. "Has your fellowship here at the Citadel seen any breakthrough in your research? Have you been able to summon anything higher than incubi?"

The younger host sadly shook his head, yet displayed a sly smile. "I assure you, no such incantation yet exists for anything beyond the common incubus and its cousins. But if there were a spell for such a calling, we would perform the ritual within a demon cell, and with appropriate magic fields in place to prevent any such conjured being from escaping." Fraughten pursed his lips and raised an eyebrow. "We aren't completely unorthodox in our ways here at the Citadel, Master Oralon."

"Of course, of course," the other replied. "But what about this...this azaribub? Does it show any potential? Is he of a higher order?"

"Doubtful. To speak to your implied question, the incubus is the most powerful demon in Hell's hierarchy that we've been able to summon. We're no further along in our research than any of the other six guilds."

Oralon tried to mask his disappointment but failed. Fraughten caught the shift in his guest's demeanour and seized it. "Now I may have a solution to this unfortunate lack of progress, if that is of any interest." The demon keeper leaned forward, seemingly eager to share this secret with his visitor.

"Yes," Oralon said, leaning in as well. "What is it?"

"In my humble opinion, it will fundamentally alter the relationship of our seven fellowships."

"Oh? How so?"

The younger mage paused, hesitated, and spoke imploringly. "First, I need your assurance, Master Oralon, that you will keep this in the strictest confidence. If my colleagues knew that I was conspiring with a Master from Fort Courlon, they would have my neck."

The visiting mage smiled smugly, drained his wine sipper, and poured himself another glass of port. He motioned for Fraughten to continue. "I'm listening."

The Citadel's demon keeper picked up his crystal wine glass, still full from the first pouring. "Frankly, my dear friend, as a more experienced sorcerer than myself, I am in need of your assistance."

"Of course, a'course," the fat blowhard slurred.

The younger magician smiled and said in a low voice, "The Citadel is a modest fellowship, as you know. Your guild is as humble as ours. But what if together we combined our research, our resources. Fort Courlon together with the Citadel. What if we developed a mutual, more powerful theurgy, shared our guarded incantations with one another in order to create a new spell to summon the higher devils..."

Fraughten let the implications hang in the air. Oralon put

down his wine glass and stared at his host with utter confusion.

"That is your solution to the lack of progress among the Manors? Surely this has already been discussed among our Guild Masters. You and I—meaning no offence, Fraughten—are mere servants of our greater fellowships." The older, fatter mage spoke as if to a child. "You, a demon keeper; myself, a potions master. We are mere worker bees in the larger hive of our society, if I may draw upon such a metaphor. To enter into such talks as you intimate is quite beyond our level of responsibility."

The thin magician took on a faraway look. "And yet, you came today to inspect our captured azaribub at my invitation. Upon your own admission at your arrival, this visit is not an official one. You volunteered to come. Out of your own desire, you wanted to see what the Citadel has in its prison pits. And now, I've piqued your curiosity, have I not?"

"Well..."

"The prospect of a larger role in this *hive* of ours, isn't that an intriguing possibility to you? That we might be true decision makers rather than mere cogs in a wheel?"

With a slight nod, the guest admitted the truth of it.

"You see, Master Oralon, I believe deep down you desire what I do, what all talented but unrecognised Masters desire. Honour, respect, fame. You want to be a man of import, do you not?"

Another slight nod, another long swallow of port. Fraughten put down his glass untasted and continued his speech.

"And yet cataloguing herbs and portioning out potions, or in my case, taking care of a few demons, feeding them animal bones like a common zookeeper, aren't these tasks beneath our abilities? We do the grunt work while our so called betters receive the glory?"

Oralon belched and said a bit forcefully, "You are quite blunt in your assessment of our relative positions, sir."

"Yet, what if I, a mere humble demon keeper, have conceived of a breakthrough to call forth and tether a higher demon?"

There entered a silence between them. In the long waiting, a chill crept back into the room. Fraughten got up to stoke the fire. He poured his guest some more wine. The demon keeper was patient, mindful of the war taking place within the heart and soul of his guest.

Finally, Oralon spoke, quite slowly now. "I sense from your reference to a 'breakthrough' that the matter of mutual cooperation begins with *us*?" A knowing smile formed at the corner of the drunk man's fleshy lips.

"As do our mutual benefits."

"Quite so. Hmm. Tethering a higher level demon would be quite...advantageous. To us, first. Then to our guilds." The mage from Fort Courlon downed the last of his wine in one full swig.

"Is this of interest, my dear friend?"

Fraughten's guest nodded drunkenly, his eyelids heavy but eager for details. "So that is our goal, eh? To call up a beelzebul, or even a djinni. Together, you and I? It seems all but impossible."

"Ah, but the breakthrough I speak of makes it possible. No one in the Citadel is aware of my experiments. For my work to continue, however, well, it is beyond my humble capabilities. I have need of a potions master like yourself, Oralon. You hold the key to my breakthrough. To *our* breakthrough. I want to work with you, sir."

The familiar address did not jolt the old magician this time. Instead, he felt a wave of pride wash over him, a sense of entitlement, even.

"Your own potions mage... Master Mattadorn?"

"A man lacking vision. Unlike yourself."

Oralon pushed himself up and slowly paced the circumference of the room, deep in thought, nodding and sometimes muttering to himself. The war inside him, Fraughten saw, was almost won. The guest from Fort Courlon was simply marshaling the courage and assembling the rationalizations needed for his conscious mind to make the decision. Would he throw in his lot with a member of a rival guild? Finally, the older man nodded yes, as the younger sorcerer had planned and assumed he would.

"What can I do to assist you, Fraughten? I am willing and able. What resources of mine might be of benefit in our mutual task?"

Master Fraughten got up, took the now near empty decanter of port, and poured his new associate another full glass.

"Just your willing heart, Master Oralon. Just your willing heart. As to the exact nature and details of the research, we'll get to those momentarily, I assure you. But first, let us drink a toast to our new partnership. To tame a demon."

"To tame a demon," Oralon echoed, clinking crystal with Fraughten's untouched glass.

After putting up with about five minutes of the fat man's snoring, Fraughten got up from his cushioned chair and opened the door to his library. He walked the long hall to the wooden doors that led to the demon pits. Taking the burnished key from an inner pocket of his velvet robe, he unlocked the upper level entrance to the dungeon. He recited a short incantation releasing a force field below and waited at the top of the stairs.

Up from the darkened deep, the azaribub flew. The devil landed beside the magician, its wings waving angelically, fully extended. All seven feet of its lithe but powerful, gleaming ruby red body quivered in anticipation of the sorcerer's command.

"Retrieve the fat bastard from my study and take him to your pit."

In an instant, the demon obeyed and sped to the fireside room. It returned with Master Oralon cradled in its arms like a sleeping child. The man was still snoring. Fraughten walked down the steps, and the azaribub flew past him to the Citadel's prison cells.

When the younger mage arrived, Oralon was laying at the bottom of the demon's cistern, just starting to stir. The devil flew up and landed on the observation platform next to its temporary master. Fraughten spoke a brief spell, and the air shimmered at the top of the pit, the protection barrier back in place.

"This egotistical fool was easier to manipulate than the acolyte from Manor Hunesthall."

The demon merely grunted, its devilish vocal cords made human speech difficult. Nevertheless, it growled out, "Keep your promise."

"You will come untethered once the exchange is made," came the response. "I first want to make sure the incantation you gave me works."

"Demons never lie."

"So *you* say."

By this time, Master Oralon's eyes were open. He blinked and took in his surroundings in confusion. Slowly getting up, he brushed himself off and stared up at his captor.

"Wha— what is this? Where am I?" he squeaked, panic quickly releasing him from his stupor. "Fraughten! Get me out of here. What in the devil's name are you playing at?" The older man's face was flushed now with anger.

"In the *devil's* name, I'm making an exchange, you old fool."

"How do you mean?"

"The breakthrough I mentioned. The physics of Hell work similarly to that of Earth; the conservation of energy requires an exchange. If a minor demon escapes from the pits of Hades, a human soul must replace it. Purgatory exists for this reason, Master Oralon. Haven't your lessons in theurgy taught you anything?" The younger mage let loose a spiteful laugh.

"A dead man's finger or toe is all that is necessary, not a soul..."

"Yes, yes. But a dead man's bones can only purchase the power of imps and incubi and succubi and such. To summon and tether an azaribub, for example, requires quite a bit more. A willing human, one with power. Like a beginning sorcerer."

"You mean the young initiate from Manor Hunesthall?" Oralon asked, incredulously.

Fraughten allowed himself a devilish smile. "He served his purpose. To summon a higher devil, a beelzebul for example, well, I think you know what more is required for such a task."

Realization hit the potions master like a hammer to an anvil. "Absolutely not. I have to be a willing subject." The fat mage sputtered, moving to the side of the pit, testing its walls. He spoke an incantation that had no effect.

"Save your breath. This demon cell is impervious to magic of any kind. As for being a willing subject, you came to the Citadel of your own free will and agreed to assist me in whatever manner you could. We toasted and sealed the bargain to tame a demon."

The man actually began to scream and Fraughten rolled his eyes in exasperation. "Come now, Oralon. Such desperate behaviour is beneath you."

But the prisoner continued to cry and bellow and mutter incantations until he was half spent. When the mage finally ran out of steam and bent over in exhaustion, the younger magician continued his lecture.

"The other part of the breakthrough came when I stumbled upon something quite intriguing. In exchange for gaining its freedom, the previous incubus we held here at the castle offered me an incantation. It said it would summon a devil like itself, but more powerful. We could never command such a thing from a demon, but of its own volition - and with my bonded promise of freedom - it gave me the incantation."

Fraughten let the words sink in.

"Standing beside me is the result. As you can see, the azaribub is not at all 'near the bottom of the hierarchy, akin to the imp, lacking intelligence and moral reasoning,' if I may quote you, sir."

The prisoner merely choked back a sob.

"Now we are ready for the next phase of our experiment. This creature has given me the formula for a beelzebul. And you are the necessary theurgical object Hell wants in exchange. It's really quite beautiful in its simplicity, don't you think?"

Arazon started to scream again, but a movement from the younger sorcerer's fingers and a magical word sent the older mage to the ground, whimpering in pain. Laying in a heap, he quietly begged for mercy. Without deigning a reply, Fraughten began the spell.

Words flowed, almost tangible in nature, and the atmosphere grew heavy with pressure as the boundaries between the phenomenal and the noumenal worlds expanded, touched, and penetrated one another. The air suddenly chilled. For Hell, though identified with fire and brimstone because of the acrid flame that demons spit, is actually a frigid, barren, isolated place. The demon pit filled with an expanse of brilliant blue light, and the old magician was lifted from the ground. His cries became shrieks as he started spinning at the center of his prison. Faster and faster the man twisted, his arms and legs and robe flailing in the violent vortex created by the intersecting dimensions.

The final words of Fraughten's incantation matched the volume of the increasingly loud phenomena occurring in front of him. With a sudden shout, the spell was cast, the summoning made, the magic released.

In the next instant, the exchange was made. Below, in the now darkened pit, stood a beelzebul. The demon's black scales shimmered, reflecting back what little light there was in the cavern. The azaribub, untethered at last, sped for the exit, its red scaled wings flapping with aberrant pleasure. Fraughten, unconcerned about the loosed demonspawn, gazed into the upturned face of his new prisoner with maniacal glee.

Staring back were the glowing, vengeful eyes of a here-to-fore unseen Hell-born specimen, the second highest ranking demon in the hierarchy of Hades. That is, if the fleeing azaribub could be believed. The magnificent devil immediately launched itself upward, springing from his hind legs with a force that would take him through the highest roof of the Citadel.

Except its escape was thwarted completely as it smashed head first into the magical barrier that kept it bound. The devilish beast plummeted back to the bottom of its dungeon pit.

Fraughten was pleased. The field had shimmered and hummed but had held fast. Even a djinni could not escape from such a powerfully enchanted stronghold. The magician laughed and stretched his arms wide. "You're tethered to me, demon. Do you accept your fate?"

The fallen spirit spit out a blazing flame of fire that hit the upper field and dissipated. The beelzebul roared and turned its eight foot frame into a chaotic whirlwind of might and fury. It lashed out at the moss covered walls; it tried to dig into the barren earth below; it flew straight up into the force field again and again.

Once more, the captured demon let out a howl of anger and madness that echoed throughout the crypt. Fire erupted from its throat and lightning sparks flew from its clawed finger tips. The smell of burnt sulfur and the stench of death filled the cavern.

It was all to no avail. The demon prison held fast.

"You can speak, I imagine. Give me your answer." Fraughten's voice was firm and bold with command.

The sides of the beelzebul heaved with seething anger, but the devil remained silent.

"Demon! Do you accept your fate?"

Finally, it nodded once, and a hateful *yesssss* escaped its deadly lips. Now came the bargaining. For its freedom, the lesser azaribub had given up the secret incantation needed to summon this beelzebul. Would this more powerful demon do the same so that Fraughten might conjure one of the mightiest of all within Hades' walls?

He could only hope.

"One more exchange, and I'll have my djinni," Fraughten muttered to himself, already knowing which of the Seven Guild Masters on the Great Council he would target for his final experiment. He would get his revenge. He'd been mocked and despised, laughed at and ridiculed for his aspirations of joining their ranks. It did not matter now. He was beyond them, yet they would regret their mockery.

The young but mighty sorcerer acknowledged his new charge. "Good. Very good. You've agreed to serve me." He rubbed his hands together in furious delight. "Now, O Demon, would you like to be set free?"

The dangerous beelzebul narrowed its eyes in suspicion.

As the evil sorcerer explained what he had in mind, the deadly devil silently considered the offer...

THE FEAST OF FOOLS

- Robert Poyton

I.

"**D**eath lurks in the shadows of the Red Palace!" The old woman's milky eyes gazed up into Llorc's face as she gripped his forearm tightly.

"And how do you know the palace is my destination?" the tall warrior asked.

"Many come here with notions of finding fame and fortune. Most get nothing more than a knife in the back and a watery grave. But you travel the silver streets with purpose. And hidden things are uncloaked to those with the Sight, young man." She released her grip.

"Yet you failed to notice the two cut-purses I just saw off." Llorc arched an eyebrow.

The woman laughed. "The Sight is a strange thing, as much affliction as blessing. And if the years have taught me anything, it is that we tend to be most blind when it comes to ourselves. But you have my gratitude, young man, which is why I give you this warning."

The pair stood bathed in the flare of a wall torch in a quiet alleyway in Virdenze. Unusually quiet, given it was the Festival of Fools and the city teemed with revelers. Indeed, that was the reason Llorc had chosen this time to carry out a task long overdue. He was here to kill the Grand Inquisitor.

Access to the city had been easy. Llorc simply joined the crowds travelling across the causeway that led to the single gate. Virdenze was situated in a large lagoon on the north-east Tyrr coast; a focal point on the major trade routes, and a location that had brought the city riches. Now it was home to many influential mercantile families, making it one of the most powerful city states in the region. That wealth bought some autonomy from the Emperor, though less from his priesthood; for the Inquisition held sway across the entire empire. Now, though, it was *carnivale*, a time of candle-lit parades, street performances, gambling, and masquerades. A time when the festival mask conferred anonymity on plotter, reveler and adulterer alike. For three days, the mighty and the low rubbed shoulders in the plazas and narrow thoroughfares between the canals. For three days normal rules were overturned, and a Fool was crowned Prince of Virdenze. It was a time when even the dread Inquisition momentarily relaxed their grip. What better opportunity for an outland assassin to make his move?

Llorc had been making his way to the Red Palace, home of the Inquisitor, when he'd come across the pair of bullies threatening the old charm seller. One now lay dead in the reeking alley, the other fled into the murky night.

"Death in the shadows, you say?" he cleaned and sheathed his poniard.

"Yes. The treasures of the Inquisition are never unguarded."

Llorc grunted. Such had been his experience. Since leaving his frozen northern homeland and wandering the civilisations to the south he had rarely found anything of value left unwatched, even offerings to the dead. He suppressed a shudder as he recalled the spider-haunted tombs of distant Sahkmet, then, flicking back his long, black hair, he glanced around.

"I thank you for the warning, though it is not treasures I seek. But we should leave this place. That idiot may return with friends."

The charm seller nodded. "You are right. I can find my way back to the busier areas. And you, warrior? If I were younger I might invite you to my rooms, perhaps?"

"And if I were older I might take you up on the offer!" Llorc smiled.

The woman's laughter echoed his as he strode away towards the lights at the end of the alleyway.

The street was crowded, a jostling throng flowing steadily towards the centre of festivities. Most were costumed, all wore a mask of some description. Llorc donned his own plain mask, raised the hood of his dark blue cloak and slid into the stream of revelers. Even in such a cosmopolitan group, he stood out. Taller than most, wide at the shoulder, lithe and compact in his movements. But it was his eyes that drew most attention. Cold and grey they were, in a high cheek-boned face. His pale skin was darkened by southern suns, his hair worn long in the manner of his people.

Although speaking many tongues, his accent also betrayed his northern origins. For Llorc was a son of the Clannacht, a warrior of the Wolf Clan - though, unlike his totem, he most often hunted alone. The cloak concealed a light leather jerkin, dark linen breeches and a long poniard at the belt. Few save nobility went openly armed in the city, and Llorc had no desire to draw the attention of the militia.

He allowed the crowd to carry him the way he wanted to go, towards the far edge of the city. Through the labyrinthine streets they swept, crossing canals at narrow, single arched bridges, traversing small, torch-lit squares, coming at last into the main plaza. In this large, open space mummers pranced, jugglers performed and lutists strolled, singing. Children laughed and darted about, the voices of sweating revelers were coarse and harsh in the thick air. The aroma of cooking meat mingled with the fragrance of incense from large censers dotted around the perimeter. And under it all lurked the ever pervasive damp-rot stench of the canals. Llorc brushed aside the furtive approach of a dream flower seller and pushed through to the far end of the plaza. There it was; the Red Palace, squatting at the centre of its watery web.

A broad stair swept up to a large black wooden door, studded with iron. A line of palace guard was positioned across the steps, each man sweating in his open face helm and curaisse, each man armed with a pike and sword. *No way in there, then*, Llorc thought. He bought some shapeless scraps of meat from a vendor and took the opportunity to stand in a shadowed corner, observing the building as he tilted the mask to stuff the spicy slivers into his mouth. The building was large and square, three stories high with turreted corner towers. It was made of a stone quarried far to the south, Llorc had heard. It was the red hue of this stone that gave the palace its name, though there were darker rumours. In the dawn light the palace blazed crimson, they said. Here, at night, in the ruddy torch glow the stone was the colour of old, spilled blood.

The palace was situated on the edge of the plaza overlooking the lagoon. The only entrance appeared to be here at the front, through presumably there would be some sort of dock at the rear. Llorc wiped greasy fingers on his cloak and moved a little closer to the steps. The lower windows were mere slits, offering no egress to a man of his size. Windows in the upper floors were wide, though barred. Over those loomed gargoyles, casting sneers and grimaces across the throng below. Llorc drew back at the sound of voices and tramping feet behind him. A group of lightly armoured militia were approaching, two bound figures in their midst. The leader of the squad marched halfway up the steps and Llorc positioned himself to overhear the conversation.

"Prisoners?" called down the central figure atop the steps.

"Aye, Captain," called the leader of the squad. "It's chaos as usual. Our cells are full to overflowing. Prefect Caprenius bade us bring these prisoners here. He said they can rest in the Inquisition cells."

The Captain grinned and stepped aside. "Good luck to them. They'll be lucky to see daylight again, whatever their misdemeanours!"

The group trotted up the steps, the prisoners struggling against their bonds in fear. The staves of the militia drove them through the door, which briefly opened to allow access, then slammed shut with grim finality behind them. Llorc grinned.

He'd found his way in.

II.

The militia sergeant sighed, motioned to the Prefect and pointed across the smoky tavern room.

"That one," he whispered. Caprenius craned his neck to take in the tall, broad figure sprawled in a chair, flagon held aloft, two senseless militia-men at his feet.

"More ale," roared the man, the hapless innkeeper rushing over to refill the mug.

"How many men do you have?" asked the portly Caprenius, stroking his goatee beard.

"After those two, only three more and myself." The sergeant indicated the nervous men behind him. "What should we do?"

Caprenius coughed and loosened his collar. "Why, go and arrest him, sergeant, go and arrest him! I'll supervise from here."

Minutes later Llorc was restrained. Much to the relief of the militia-men he had put up little struggle. Perhaps in deference to that, he escaped the beating that most prisoners received and was taken in haste to the Red Palace.

Llorc grit his teeth at the cuff round the head and shove of the guard. He allowed himself to stumble against the far wall and slither to the floor in apparent drunken terror. With a clang, the bars shut behind him and the warrior was left to take in his surroundings. A small cell, dimly lit by a torch in the corridor outside. Filthy straw on the floor, a rank smelling bucket in the corner. No cot, nor any concession to prisoner comfort. He smiled. All was as expected, with the added bonus of being alone. He had taken a chance on the Inquisition cells being single-occupant, given that the usual guest here would be heretic rather than drunkard. Reaching into his boot, he pulled out the thin lock-pick. He wore only breeches and linen shirt, the rest of his gear was back at the tavern, the innkeeper paid well to store it and to tend his horse.

Llorc turned his attention to the lock. A decade or so ago, as a youth new to civilisation, he'd run with the gangs of the Ratteries in Adelphis. The skills learnt there had not left him and, with a soft click, the door swung open. Llorc spared little glance for the occupants of neighbouring cells, huddled drunks for the most part. As much as he would free anyone from the clutches of the Inquisition, he had not the time to release all. His entire will was focused on the death of the man called Tolomeo. Crossing the corridor, he glided soundlessly up the steps, drawn to the light and voices drifting through the half open door above. The gaoler, a sallow, pinched-faced individual, was grumbling to his companion, an elderly servant who had carried in a platter of food.

"This is all I get, is it?" The gaoler was complaining. "Upstairs they dine on the finest fowl and wines and I get bread and water? I might as well be one of those in the cells."

"Keep complaining and you might be," was the servant's dry retort before leaving the guard room. Llorc was across the room in three strides, dealing the gaoler a buffet to the head. The man was knocked from his stool, unconscious before he hit the ground. Leaving him bound and gagged, the warrior peered around the door opposite. At the end of the passage lay another flight of upward steps. These led Llorc up to the servants area of the palace, a hive of activity typical of that which underpins all such edifices. The activity worked in Llorc's favour. Staff were coming and going at such a pace that none looked twice at the tall figure lurking in the shadows. A huge kitchen was the hub of the ants nest, and from overheard conversations, the lurker gathered that a social event of some kind was in progress upstairs. Grabbing a large, silver platter from a nearby pile, he straightened his shirt, brushed the straw from his hair and chanced the next set of stairs.

Things were more dangerous here. The upstairs servants were of the more observant kind. Butlers, footmen, stewards, guiding costumed guests, chiding tardy serving staff and, Llorc noticed, checking invitations. He cursed under his breath and ducked back into an alcove as a particularly strident steward bustled past. Salvation came when he espied a liveried servant exiting a small door concealed in the panelling opposite. *Perhaps this led to living quarters, perhaps even to the private chambers of the Inquisitor General.* Llorc waited for the corridor to clear then, swift as the hunting wolf, was across the open space, through the door, and gone.

The narrow staircase beyond opened into a carpeted passageway softly lit by a large lantern. From the left drifted the hum of conversation and the rhythmic pulse of music. To the right the corridor ended in a dark wooden door. The sudden sound of an approaching voice drove Llorc to it. Slipping inside, he found himself in a small suite of finely furnished chambers. Candlelight revealed a decor that was sober but luxurious; dark rugs, heavy red hangings and finely carved, solid, black furniture. The voice grew louder and Llorc hastened through the archway opposite and into the adjoining chamber, doing his best to conceal himself behind a pair of thick curtains. The door opened and feet shuffled across the rugs. The voice could be heard clearly now.

"And at the sounding of the gong you are to bring the girl to Master Tolomeo at the upstairs ritual chamber. Understand?"

"Yes, Your Worship."

"His Eminence attends his guests at present but it is vital that the ritual go ahead at the prescribed time."

"Of course, Your Worship."

"Ensure there is a plentiful supply of wine for our guests and once you have delivered the girl, be sure to inform all servants and staff to remain below stairs. Clear?"

"Clear, Your Worship. And the guards?"

"They are to remain on the doors. No-one comes in, no-one goes out. Very well. Attend to the girl now, keep her calm. The last thing we need is that brat screaming her head off."

The door creaked again and Llorc risked a peek through the gap. A tall man stood in the other chamber, his back to Llorc, pouring wine into a silver goblet. He wore a long robe of deep purple, a matching skullcap atop his shaved scalp.

Without hesitation Llorc bounded from his hiding place and pounced, wrapping one brawny arm around the man's neck, clasping his hands together at his victim's shoulder. The man gave a choking cry, dropping the goblet with a clatter, red wine running across the table top. Wiry hands came up to grab Llorc's forearm, to no avail. Llorc dragged his prey backwards, the man's heels drumming on the rug. The struggles grew weaker as he was pulled through the archway and by the time the pair reached the far wall, the robed figure was limp and senseless. Llorc squeezed for a little longer to be sure, then released his grip, letting the man slide to the floor. Flipping him over with the toe of his boot, Llorc got his first proper look at his victim. A severe face looked at up at him, middle aged, the mouth set in what appeared to be a permanent down-turn. Llorc recognised the garb and paraphernalia from previous encounters. This man was an Inquisitor.

Knowing that, Llorc was not too gentle in his actions. He swiftly divested the cleric of his robes, taking also the blank, white mask that hung from the belt. He slipped the garment over his head. The man was roughly the same height as Llorc but somewhat slighter in stature; the robe pinched across the shoulders but would have to do for now.

Llorc tucked his hair inside the raised cowl and positioned the mask. A quick search of the room revealed thick braided ties at the curtains, which he used to bind the man at wrist and ankle. A kerchief from the man's pocket served as a gag and, thus restrained, Llorc rolled the unconscious form behind a couch in the corner and returned to the corridor, heading towards the music.

The masque was the highlight of the social year, attended by all those of import, or who wished to be thought of as important. The costumes here were elaborate and expensive, each vying to outdo the other. A quartet played at one end of the large ballroom, the air was thick with chatter and the scent of exotic perfumes. Llorc navigated the room slowly, trying to avoid eye contact, conversation, or bumping into anyone. He was aided in this by his distinctive garb; few, it seemed, cared to engage an Inquisitor in small talk. Couples whirled and span across the floor, colourful silks rustled, ornate headdresses bobbed. Golden animal faces leered, dark eyes flashed behind bejewelled half-masks. A horned, demonic grimace loomed and was gone. Another reveler swept past, cloaked in scarlet, a death's head grinning beneath the wide-brimmed, plumed hat.

Llorc muttered under his breath and edged to the peripheries, taking position before a long table piled high with platters of food. There came a peal of laughter and squeals of delight as a capering, dwarfish jester pulled on a silver chain, leading a figure dressed in an ornate ape costume into the centre of the room. The great and the good flirted, dined, drank, danced and guffawed. Llorc took stock of the wide doorway opposite, flanked by liveried footmen, which, he judged, must lead towards the heart of the building. He felt sweat trickle down his back as he made his way through the throng to pass swiftly through the opening. One of the footmen gave a quizzical glance. Llorc ignored it and pressed on, relieved to see a large staircase ahead.

Bring the girl upstairs, the priest had said. Presumably that was where his superior was to be found. Llorc passed a giggling couple on the stairs. but this part of the palace appeared much quieter. The upper corridor, lined with doors, was empty. Llorc swore; he could be here all night, searching these rooms. Moving to the nearest he pressed an ear to the door, then, on hearing nothing, carefully opened it. An empty bed-chamber, a guest room, perhaps? The next four doors revealed the same, then came an intersection. Llorc paused to peer left and right before moving swiftly across to the next door. No sound. The room beyond was larger though, and richly furnished. A sliver of light glinted through a curtained archway opposite. *Could these be the chambers of the Grand Inquisitor?*

Llorc shut the door and padded across the carpet, head thrust forward, every sense alert. A young voice hummed a tune from beyond the drapes. He glanced through the gap. A girl, perhaps seven years old, sat at a small desk, humming as she toyed with a crude doll. Despite Llorc's stealth the girl turned, her pale face framed by dark curls. She frowned and spoke.

"Who's there? Who is that?"

Llorc stepped into the inner chamber and held his palms up. The girl slipped off the chair and peered up at him.

"Who are you? You are not Grimani, though you wear his robes."

Llorc removed the mask and knelt, smiling. "Fear not, little one. I'm not here to harm you."

"No," replied the girl, frown deepening. "You are here to kill my father."

III.

Llorc was taken aback. *Did the girl have some sort of sorcerous gift? Could she hear his thoughts?* He was at a loss to reply and settled on a shrug.

"What is your name?" he eventually responded.

"My name is Masina," she replied cautiously. "What's yours?"

"I am Llorc. And why do you think I mean harm to your father?"

The girl's reply was interrupted by the sound of the outer door opening. Llorc stood, wheeling, pulling aside the curtain.

Before him stood the footman from the ballroom, who pointed and said to his companion, "See, I was right! I thought something was wrong! We have a rogue in the house!"

The guard at his side snarled, stepping forward as he drew the short sword at his belt, hissing, "Sound the alarm, I'll deal with this idiot."

With a rush he was on Llorc, who ducked the first swing and hurled himself at the armed man. Grabbing his attacker round the waist Llorc pulled him to the floor, reaching for the guard's sword arm. The pair tussled, Llorc cursing at the restricting robes that clutched at his movement. His attacker's confidence suddenly ebbed as he felt the power in the iron grip on his wrist, followed by another that closed around his throat. The guard attempted to scream and began to frantically writhe. To no avail, Llorc was now in control. *But how long before the footman returned with reinforcements?* As the man beneath him spluttered his last, Llorc was suddenly aware of the footman backing into the room, hands held protectively before him.

"No! No! Please!" the liveried servant cried in vain, as another figure stepped through the doorway to thrust a long knife into his chest. The footman fell, blood blossoming across his doublet as the newcomer kicked the door shut and stood glaring down at the pair before her.

"Who the hell are you?" she hissed. The woman wore simple servant garb, removing her headscarf to shake free long, dark curls. Her green eyes flashed as she glanced at the girl now peering through the curtain.

"Masina!" she called, though the girl gave no response. "If you've harmed her at all!" she pointed the knife at Llorc.

"Not I. I am here for other purposes. But who are you?"

"I am Francina," came the reply. "I am the girl's mother."

As Llorc checked both bodies, Francina crossed the room to kneel before her daughter, holding her by the upper arms. She was talking softly to the girl, but to no avail. She stood and turned as Llorc approached.

"She does not know you?" he asked.

Francina wiped a hand across her eyes and shook her head. "No. I fear her mind has been clouded, or turned in some way. Damn Tolomeo!" She spat on the rug.

"The Grand Inquisitor? I don't understand. He is the girl's father?"

Francina's eyes blazed again and she stabbed a finger at Llorc. "No, he is not! My daughter was taken. Sold to the Inquisitor by my drunken sot of a husband."

Llorc eyebrows raised. He'd encountered many strange things during his time in the civilised lands, selling your own child was a new low.

"Yes, yes, I know." Francina read his expression. "That pig would do anything to fund his revels, aye, even sell his own child. By the time I found out, it was too late."

"Could you not simply demand her return?"

"Demand?" Francina scoffed. "This is Virdenze. No one demands anything of the Inquisition here. No, instead I contrived to gain employ in the palace. For the last weeks I have scrubbed floors, cleaned fireplaces, all the while seeking for news of my daughter. It was only today that I heard of a girl held in these upstairs chambers. I thought the festivities a good opportunity to find her. And now I have. But what of you? You have not told me who you are or why you are here."

"I am Llorc mac Lughaidh, of the north. A Clannacht." The names brought no recognition to Francina's face. As far as most southerners were concerned the north was a frozen wasteland inhabited by barely literate savages. "Like you, I thought this a good time to infiltrate Tolomeo's palace. But my goal is to kill the swine."

Francina gave a short laugh. "Good luck with that. And you came here unarmed? "

Llorc shrugged. "I had to, in order to be arrested." He knelt and picked up the dead guard's sword with a grin. "Besides... now I have a sword. There was mention of taking the girl up to the ritual chamber at the sound of a gong. What know you of this?"

The woman shuddered. "Goddess aid us! Dark rumours are spoken of Tolomeo. Mine is not the first child that has been taken. Some speak of evil rites, of sacrifice and devils. It seems I arrived just in time. I will take the girl and leave now, hopefully any enchantment will wear off in time."

Llorc nodded, casting aside the priest robes as Francina scooped her daughter up in her arms. They were barely back out in the corridor when a sound drifted up from below that froze the blood in their veins; it was the repeated chiming of a large gong. Llorc ran to the head of the stairs and cursed.

"Back the other way," he called. "People are coming up the stairs."

The pair fled back along the corridor, eventually finding a smaller staircase that led upwards. Shouts sounded, the girl's disappearance having been discovered, it seemed. Without pause, Llorc took the stairs ahead, holding the short sword he'd taken from the guard before him. He burst onto a large landing, surprising the two guards stationed at a doorway opposite. With a snarl, Llorc hurled himself forward, plunging the sword into the belly of the first guard before he'd even time to draw his weapon.

The second man was quicker. He drew and slashed in one smooth motion, forcing Llorc back onto his heels. Again the guard slashed but Llorc was ready this time. He dropped, one hand supporting himself on the carpeted floor, the other whipping out to slice into the side of his attacker's knee. With a cry the guard stumbled, Llorc quickly finishing him off with a stab to the chest.

Francina was behind him now, the girl resting quietly in her arms. She gave barely a glance at the two prone figures slumped in expanding pools of blood, muttering, "There's more noise downstairs. They'll be up here soon."

Llorc cursed and glanced around. Ahead lay only the formerly guarded door. Llorc gave a glance at Francina, she shrugged. Llorc turned the handle and pushed the heavy, creaking portal open. The thick scent of strange incense drifted out to greet him, the curtains across the threshold blocking any view. He thrust his head through the heavy purple drapes, teeth gritted, sword at the ready. The chamber was large, its walls panelled with dark oak, its corners concealed in shadows. He took in at once the low, circular dais at its centre, a lectern at its far side, beyond which hung more drapes. The ruddy glow of coals radiated from three shallow bowls positioned around the dais. As Llorc moved forward, he noticed rugs on the wooden floor, a table, bookcases and a pair of tall cabinets at the outer edges of the lambent glow. Francina followed, closing the door and drawing the heavy interior bolt with a clunk. Twenty paces brought them to the platform. It was a single step high, a large circle drawn at its centre, its circumference ringed with strange symbols. Llorc's nape bristled.

"Sorcery," he muttered, eyes flicking around the room. Francina gasped and stepped back. "The symbols! If you look at them, they move... they squirm!"

"Best not look. Let's see if we can find you a way out of this stone barn. Then I can do what I came here to do." He gestured towards the curtains beyond the dais. "This way."

IV.

Llorc's movement towards the far end of the chamber was brought short by the appearance of a tall, gaunt figure through the drapes. A man in sable robes, his shaven pate and bone-white skin lending him the aspect of a skull, entered.

"Ah, Grimani, place the girl in the centre of the circle, would you. I - " His instructions were cut off as he looked up. Dark eyes blazed as he took in the intruders.

"Tolomeo!" hissed Francina, hand dropping to the knife at her belt. Llorc grinned and strode forward. Any confusion experienced by the Grand Inquisitor quickly vanished. He gestured and uttered a single syllable that smote the pair like a physical blow. Llorc was immediately halted in his tracks, held in the grip of some unseen force. Francina reeled back, tucking her shoulders in to protect the girl in her arms before slumping to floor.

The Inquisitor strode confidently forward to examine them, as though each were some peculiar specimen in a collection.

"What have we here?" his voice was soft and raspy, like the skitter of dead leaves across flagstones. "Ah, the girl. You would be the mother, I presume? And you," he turned to view Llorc. "You must be the father. But no." His thin eyebrows creased. "You have the appearance of a mere ruffian but there is something else about you. How curious."

Llorc spoke through gritted teeth, sweat dripping from his brow as he fought against the invisible grasp.

"Release me and I'll show you exactly what I am, dog. Your doom!"

Tolomeo took this news with no sign of perturbation. "So a common assassin, then? Nothing interesting at all. Who sent you? Dario? Afani? Montresor, perhaps? No, I see no sign of recognition in you at any of these names."

"I have my own motives, dead man."

"I'm sure you do. But as you have just discovered, a Grand Inquisitor is not so easy to kill."

The harsh bark of laughter raised an eyebrow. "Your predecessor, Maldovio, died easily enough."

A look of surprise flashed across the pale features. "You knew him? You were at the Siege of Arilarat?"

"Aye, I was there." Llorc spoke with effort, lips writhing. "A mercenary in the employ of the knights of your Order. One of the few that faced the Jahari hoards. Life was perilous enough before your murdering Inquisition arrived. "

Tolomeo stepped closer to his captive. "Maldovio never returned from that place. You had a hand in this? You killed him?"

"He perished not at my hand, though I sorely wished it.

No, he died at the hands of the wretches we freed from his care. They served their own justice on your friend. Like most of you civilised men, he could give pain but not take it."

"Heathen swine!" The Inquisitor's face contorted into a mask of hatred. "He was a great man! You witless savage!"

Llorc's facial muscles twitched as he drew his lips back in a mirthless grin. "Savage, you say? Yet my people do not murder children."

The priest sneered. "What is the life of a guttersnipe? A small price to pay to summon those of the Outer Dark."

Francina had dragged herself forward a little and spoke with some effort. "Outer Dark? Yet you serve the Goddess, surely?"

The sneer remained. "Our office was ever a mask for our true worship. The Goddess? Kindness, honour, service? Weakness, idiocy and servility. Words for fools. The servants of the Outer Dark value prestige, wealth, power. Mastery over others, strength through fear, these are our goals." He strode to the lectern and placed his thin hands reverentially upon the aged tome that rested upon it. "The Book of Sesokris. Its acquisition was most challenging, for the Sorcerer Kings of Sahkmet guard their tombs well. But now its secrets are mine, and following tonight's ritual, all will learn to fear the shadows!"

"Monster!" Francina exclaimed. "You would unleash hell on the whole city?"

"Not hell, wench, Merely... servants. They will be summoned tonight and sent to destroy those who would oppose us. Ah, you wonder why we need your daughter? She is to provide the cords that bind the servants of the Outer Dark to my will. For blood is prized by those I would summon, the blood of the innocent even more so."

Francina used what little movement she had to clutch her daughter tightly. Tolomeo crouched now, beckoning to Masina. "Come, child. Your father calls. Come!"

To Francina's obvious distress the girl slipped from her mother's grasp and walked, wide-eyed, towards the open arms of the vulturous figure before her.

"You heartless bastard!" screamed the mother hoarsely, eliciting only a dry chuckle from the Inquisitor.

"A simple enough glamour. The girl considers me her father. Let's face it, she probably never knew her real father, anyway." He placed a proprietary hand on Masina's shoulder. Llorc strained every sinew of his being at the sight but was unable to break those unholy bonds. The drapes whispered as two robed men shuffled through, faces hidden in the shadow of their deep cowls. At Tolomeo's command they stepped forward to seize Llorc and drag him to the edge of the dais. He hissed, he spat, he cursed, but to no avail. Even the sword dropped with a thud to the floor. Yet as he was held in the grip of the two acolytes, Llorc detected a faint weakening of the sorcerous ties that bound him, for the Inquisitor had now turned his full attention to mother and child.

Tolomeo led the girl to the centre of the circle, then strode to Francina, dragging her, protesting, to sit beside her daughter. He returned to the lectern, opened the book with a dry creak, and began reading aloud from its yellowed pages. His sonorous intonations echoed weirdly around the chamber. The Inquisitor next withdrew a curved dagger and a phial of powder from the depths of his robes. He brandished the former in curious patterns as he poured the content of the latter into the flames of the nearest firebowl. A plume of lurid green smoke arose, Tolomeo now sweeping the blade as if to slice it into sections.

His voice grew louder, more urgent, the unearthly syllables jarring the ears with their harsh cadence. The foul vapours dispersed, snaking up and out to the corners of the room, though there was no draft to drive them.

Llorc relaxed his arms. The acolytes, intent on their master's actions, had loosened their grips slightly. The warrior felt some movement returning to him. Not only was the Inquisitor distracted, he also, like many accustomed to subservience, underestimated the resolve of his captive. Llorc focused his entire will on breaking free of the unseen bonds. Fingernails bit into his palms, teeth ground in soundless fury. Deep within, the hackles of the wolf rose, a low growl started that rose throughout his being, gaining in strength as the spell weakened.

As the chanting reached a peak, Llorc exploded into action. He barged one acolyte aside, grabbed the other by the scruff of the robe and sent him spinning across a firebowl. The man fell heavily across the coals, screaming as robe and skin sizzled. Next, Llorc leapt for the chanting figure, but the Inquisitor was fast. With a lithe twist he evaded Llorc's grasp and slashed out with the dagger. Llorc cursed, springing back to avoid the attack. That brought him within reach of the first acolyte, now recovered. That man hurled himself onto Llorc's back, wrapping an arm around his throat in an attempt to choke the warrior. He might as well have tried to wrestle a panther.

Llorc dropped to one knee and dipped a shoulder, sending the man flying over him to crash to the floor, where he lay stunned. But Llorc had no time to enjoy this victory as the curved dagger hissed out again, slicing his shirt this time, though not reaching the skin.

Llorc gave ground to the relentless barrage of slashes and stabs that now faced him. The Inquisitor's face was a mask of fury, eyes blazing as he forced back the object of his rage. The wavering voice of the second acolyte snapped him out of his frenzy.

"Master! The shadows! They are here!"

"Curse you!" shrieked Tolomeo, wheeling away to finish the incantation. Then, to the smouldering acolyte. "Blood! We need blood to control them. Kill the girl!"

The half-burnt figure lurched into the circle, flexing his fingers as he made for Masina. But Francina was now also free of the spell, and she threw herself at the acolyte, her own knife in hand, stabbing wildly. Her target dodged the attack and slapped her hard across the face before knocking her hand aside, sending the knife spinning out of her grasp. The man locked bony hands around Francina's throat. His face loomed in her sight, eyebrows singed, skin blistered, yellowed teeth bared in a snarl of pain and anger as he drove her back, grip tightening, tightening. She punched and hit to no avail and her vision began to darken.

Llorc swore and made for the circle but was brought up short. A vague shape descended from the darkness above to stand before him, roughly human in outline, but dim and shadowy in substance. Llorc was aware of an intelligence within the thing, or at least of a malignance that emanated from it. He shifted right and the shape matched his movement. With a snarl Llorc hurled himself forward, hoping either to pass through or to knock it aside. Neither of those things happened. The first sensation was of mind-numbing cold. Llorc had been raised in the dark, sunless forests of the north, but this cold was of another order entirely. It was the coldness of the gulf, of the total absence of heat, of light, of life itself.

The second sensation was of crushing pressure as the thing extended arms, or whatever passed for arms, around his torso. Llorc felt as though he were drowning in an icy sea. Shards of cold pierced his brain. The idea of sunlight, of warmth, became a dim and distant memory as conscious thought faded. But in place of conscious thought came instinct, the will to survive. That primal force sparked an ember of resistance and Llorc began to struggle against the dark void that beckoned him, that urged to him surrender, to just close his eyes and give in. With an effort that brought needles of pain to numb hands, Llorc tore himself free and reeled, panting, across the room. He dropped to one knee, shivering uncontrollably, but alive.

Francina was fading fast. Her attacker sat astride her, fingers clamped around her throat. But the thought of her daughter lent fresh power to her limbs and, remembering the times spent wrestling with older brothers, she placed a foot against the man's thigh and pushed it away. The acolyte fell and, using the momentum, Francina twisted, swinging a leg over to reverse their positions. The deadly grip was loosened, even more so by the fist she pounded into the side of the man's head. Something flashed at the acolyte's throat, a thick chain bearing the sign of his order. Francina bunched the links in one hand, wrenching the chain tight across the grimacing man's windpipe. Cursing in his face, she pulled hard.

The acolyte tried her own trick against her but she was prepared, lifting a supporting knee to drop it sharply into her attacker's belly. That knocked what precious little air he had out of him and the acolyte's struggles weakened. With a cry and a final jerk, Francina twisted the chain deep into the man's neck until he expired, tongue extended between darkening lips.

Panting for breath, Francina slid free and turned to her daughter. The girl sat in the centre of the circle, her mother's knife in hand. She was glancing from Tolomeo to her mother, then back to the knife. The Inquisitor was shouting.

"My daughter, listen to me. That woman before you wishes you harm. You must kill her! Stab her with the knife, your father's life depends on it."

Francina, vision blurred and swimming, could only watch with the horror as her daughter advanced upon her, knife upheld in tiny hand, a look of determined concentration on her face.

"That's it! Good girl!" cackled the Inquisitor.

Francina raised a weak hand in protest as her daughter stood over her, knife poised.

"Masina," she whispered hoarsely. "It's Mama. Listen to me, baba. It's Mama."

Masina's brow creased as the knife wavered in her hand. An internal struggle flashed across her face as she lifted the weapon higher for the killing blow. It never came. The girl suddenly slumped, dropping the blade. She looked up in confusion, as if awakening, muttering, "Mama?"

Francina stretched out, plucked the knife from the floor, flipped the grip and send it spinning towards the Inquisitor. It caught him in the shoulder and he stepped back with a cry, his vestment suddenly stained with a dark bloom of blood. Horrified realisation dawned on his face.

The thing facing Llorc darted towards Tolomeo as, like sharks scenting blood, two more shadow-forms plunged down from the gloom above. Llorc staggered across to Francina as the Inquisitor screamed at the touch of his would-be servitors. Before the pair's eyes, all heat and life slowly drained from that already pale face, the screams subsiding to whimpers, then to a low keening that gradually faded away to nothingness.

"We need to get out of here," Llorc urged. A thudding at the bolted entrance told of the discovery of slain guards and only increased their urgency.

"He came through those curtains, must be another room," Francina croaked as she rose unsteadily, one hand grasping her daughter.

But the shadow-things lay between them and the exit. And the shadow-things, now that they had drained their victim, were looking for new life to feed on. With a soft thud, Tolomeo's husk of a corpse hit the floor as the creatures turned. Again, the wave of malignance swept over Llorc, the impression of a vast hunger, of a need to absorb light, life and hope.

"Morrg!" he cursed. The short sword lay a few paces away but he felt no confidence in its use against these creatures. Still, if he had to die it would be with blade in hand. He lunged to pick up the sword and readied himself to attack. Then another thought struck him.

"What destroys the darkness?" he called to Francina. "What keeps away the cold?"

"Fire!" she replied and raced at once to the nearest bowl. She grabbed its lip, wincing at the pain in her palms, tipping the red hot coals onto the carpeted floor. The rug began smouldering immediately. Francina cast around, grabbing the book on the lectern and throwing it onto the orange heap. Its pages flickered then burst into small, violet flames. Francina continued, grabbing items from the table, paper, cloth, overjoyed at finding a small flask of oil, which she added to the growing conflagration

Llorc realised he had to buy Francina time. With a snarl he charged the shadow-things, taking the fight to the enemy as was the way of his people. As he feared, the sword did nothing. It merely cut through the things as though they were smoke, slicing them apart only for the sections to reform.

But Llorc was in his element now. As the wolf arose within, he let loose a fearsome Clannacht war-cry and redoubled his efforts. The things swarmed over him, every touch a glacial stab, every grip burning in its coldness. Llorc was fighting purely from instinct now, all rationality gone, his only aim to inflict as much damage as he could before he died. As blue sparks burst in his vision, as he cut and thrust again and again with the short sword, the world shrank to a tiny dot of life and light. Then even that was gone.

Llorc came round with Francina above him rubbing his arms, slapping his face. He heard his name being called as if from a far, distant place. The smell of burning came to his nostrils and his body turned automatically towards the heat. A fire was raging in the centre of the room, the warmth never felt so good. After what felt like an age, life returned painfully his limbs and he was able to stand.

"What…" was all he could say.

"The things were upon you. I grabbed a drape, set it aflame then hurled it at them. It drove them off, though I know not if they still lurk nearby. But we have another problem. The room is ablaze!"

Llorc nodded and, pausing only to retrieve the sword from where it had fallen, stumbled away from the scarlet and orange flames and cloying smoke that were beginning to fill the chamber. Beyond the curtained archway lay more chambers, presumably the personal rooms of the Grand Inquisitor . A window beckoned, its soft bars easily torn aside by the coughing warrior.

"The bed. Tear sheets, make strips," Llorc indicated as he glanced out of the window, taking in a lungful of sweet, night air.

"I have a small boat tethered at the rear dock," Francina explained as she tore and tied strips. "Thought I might need it to escape."

"Good thinking," Llorc grinned. His own plan had extended little further than killing his target. Tying one end of the sheet rope to the bedstead, Llorc lowered down Francina, then her daughter, before finally descending hand over hand himself. They dropped onto a small walkway at the rear of the palace, over-looking the dark, placid waters of the lagoon. Above them, the crackle of flame and the ruddy glow at the window told its own story.

"This way" urged Francina, and as the cries of alarm began

to sound throughout the palace, they fled swiftly to the boat.

V.

In a quiet alleyway the pair stopped to take stock. They had abandoned the boat, pushing it back out onto the canal they had turned into. No-one appeared to be following, though above the sounds of revels., cries of alarm could be heard from the nearby plaza. Francina clutched her daughter close, chest heaving in emotion. Llorc regained his breath and spoke.

"You are injured? Is the girl alright?"

"My hands hurt, my throat hurts, but I never felt better." Finger-shaped bruises were already forming on her neck. "And Masina is fine, aren't you, my lovely?"

"Good." Llorc glanced around. "Then we best depart this place. I doubt anyone saw us, but I'd still rather not be here if the militia begin sweeping the streets."

"Yes, you are right, we should. I go to join my family in the north. What of you?"

"My horse awaits at the tavern. I hear there's war brewing to the south again. If not, there will be war brewing somewhere. I'll find work."

"You mentioned you were a mercenary. I'm afraid I have little coin to offer you for your help."

Llorc laughed hoarsely. "None is required. I had my own reasons for wishing that cur dead - and now he is. And you found your child in time, so all is well."

"You never did say why you wanted him dead."

A shadow crossed Llorc's features as he cast his mind back. Back to a once beautiful face scarred beyond recognition; to a slender form twisted and broken by the rack; to a life ended by its own hand rather than face years of darkness and pain.

Francina, sensing his grief, laid a hand on his forearm. "She must have been very special."

"Aye," Llorc whispered. "She was." He sighed and ruffled Masina's hair, smiling at the crude doll that peeked out from the girl's jerkin. "Now. Be off with you and good luck on your travels."

Francina nodded and turned away. A last wave from the girl and the pair were gone.

Llorc spurred his horse up the ridge overlooking the lagoon. Virdenze lay below and behind. At the crest he halted his mount to turn and glance back down. Dawn's increasing glow was matched by the flickering flames of the Red Palace, its turrets just visible above the surrounding buildings. A huge pall of smoke curled lazily across the glassy waters of the lagoon as the rising sun blazed fire in the sky. Llorc turned his face back to the south, clicked his mount and rode on.

THE ROTTING GODDESS

- B Harlan Crawford

The only city of any size before one had to cross the parched wastes of the Surah-al-Khemi to reach Kairoo to the north or Nimrud to the east, Yeubedeh sprawled in an irregular clay and timber blot about the oasis that was its namesake.

Yeubedeh swarmed with merchants, bandits, thieves and moneylenders, all eager to prey upon the stream of travellers going to and fro, for Yeubedeh was the last chance for travellers to rest and equip themselves before the gruelling desert crossing, or the first to refresh themselves afterward.

In one of the whitewashed mudbrick houses of the residential quarter dwelt Gudea, a peddler of dyes and incense. Gudea himself sat at a table of lushly carved ebony, sobbing and tearing at his beard. His wife, Zylphah, was if anything more distraught than he, laying on the sandstone tiles and clinging to her husband's feet. Behind him stood Gudea's dull eyed, horse faced brother-in-law, Adad, who grinned vapidly while staring at the ample chest of the outlandish woman seated across the table.

Seanai of Ibak looked up from the dregs gathered at the bottom of her brass flagon to sneer at the lecherous Adad. Seanai was indifferent to the gaze of satyristic rakes, so long as they kept their hands to themselves. It was Gudea's display that discomfited her, the people of her tribe bore grief stoically.

"My daughter's remains will be defiled by these blasphemers!" Gudea wailed." I beg thee, outlander, recover her so that her soul might be given over to Asirat!"

"Tell me again what transpired, merchant."

Gudea wiped his face with sleeve, composing himself. With trembling hands, he took a sip of wine and continued.

"Shubure, my daughter, fell ill with fever. She did not linger and passed within the course of a day. As we lay her out in preparation for funeral, our house was invaded by acolytes of the noisome God-Slug, Lugloth, Lord of all that rots and suppurates."

"Did you resist them?"

"Adad, my wife's brother-" He indicated the horse-faced man, who now fairly quivered with libidinous zeal. "-and I contended with them as best as we were able, but we are but merchants, not soldiers. At least a dozen took us by surprise and overwhelmed us. They were naked and glazed with a noisome tallow they render from ripened cadavers, the stench of which blinds the eyes and scourges the stomach." Gudea blanched as if the memory of the described foulness assailed his innards once more. He took a draught of wine before he continued. "They know not fear or pain. What fear could our cudgels hold for those who mutilate themselves to be as smooth and sexless as their mucilaginous god? They stole Shubure's body. They will allow her mortal remains to molder for use in their unspeakable rites!"

Here the man's voice again dissolved into miserable sobbing.

"Calm yourself, man!" Seanai replied as gently as a savage of Dread Ibak was able. "Why have you brought me here to your home?"

Zylphah lifted her tear-streaked face from her husband's feet to issue a sobbing reply.

"After the theft, I partook of an infusion of Iaskka and other herbs, and communicated with Asirat, Glorified and Exalted. Asirat granted me a vision of a shock-headed giantess who would deliver us from our plight. Great Asirat, resplendent in her Coat of Fifty Thousand Plumes, spoke from her Celestial Palace of Eternity and told me that this giantess would be granted the hallowed might to contend with Lugloth's minions."

Zylphah buried her face in her husband's burnoosed thigh and resumed her lamentations. Gudea stroked her hair and took up the narrative.

"Hearing this from the lips of Zylphah, foremost and most treasured of my wives, I scoured the city. At the Inn of All Serpents, where foreigners are wont to gather, and I saw you, towering a head above the men of Yeubedeh with a crown of unruly ebon hair. This, I thought, could only be she who was prophesied by Asirat!"

Seanai grimaced. "I am a wanderer and vagabond. Sometimes a bandit and thief. No god would be so cruel as to point their followers my way. Further, unsettling accounts of Lugloth and his adherents drip from the lips of taletellers and scandalmongers from Kairoo to Pyun-Tai. I find it unwise to contend with devils."

Sighing heavily, Gudea rose and went to a heavy chest that lay near the wall behind him. Operating the three locks and six latches securing it, he drew forth a leather purse and laid it before Seanai.

"All I have is yours, barbarian, if you will but heed the words of Asirat, Glorified and Exalted, and bring our daughter back, whatever her state."

Seanai gazed around Gudea's modest home. It was comfortable, but not rich. There was much brass and iron, but little gold. The grunts of sheep and dromedaries could be heard from the adjoining stable. A heavy redolence of sickly-sweet incense fought to mask the scent of the livestock, and other less identifiable stinks.

Seanai picked up the purse and palpated it in the manner of one selecting a well ripened fruit. The purse was heavily gravid with orichalcum drakims. The Ibakeen rose from the table and addressed Gudea.

"I will go to this temple. With these drakims, perhaps I can buy back your girl's corpse. Many zealots become less zealous when coins touch their palm. In the meantime, seek peace. If your Asirat is a decent sort of goddess she will not punish your daughter for the actions of slug-worshipers."

"Do not invoke The Golden Lady thus, barbarian, lest you incur her wrath before facing these fiends."

Shrugging, Seanai went to the front door where awaited the leering Adad holding the great war-ax she had left in the antechamber. She took it from his hands. Scowling at Adad's greasily lubricious countenance, she spoke to Gudea.

"I will do what I can to fetch your Shubure back. When I return, give me a dromedary and enough provisions to see me to Nimrud and we can call the matter settled." Pulling her burnoose over her head, she stepped out into the street.

Presently, Seanai returned to the Inn of All Serpents, where she used a portion of Gudea's drakims to pay for a jug of unwatered wine and a bath. She paid an additional premium for the latter to include soap and nimble-fingered attendants. She did not feel Gudea would begrudge her. She would be careful to retain enough drakims to buy back a day-old corpse from the slug worshipers.

Suitably refreshed and having availed herself of a few more of Gudea's drakims to purchase a vest of boiled leather and pantaloons of red silk to replace her filthy, threadbare linen tunic, she made her way to the quarter of the town reserved for temples and houses of worship. Yeubedeh was quite tolerant of all religions, allowing the construction of temples, proselytising, and any other activity so long as it did not impinge on the conduct of business. The followers of Lugloth, with their disturbing rites and proclivities with rancid human cadavers, were skating dangerously close to violating this one unignorable sin but were still tolerated for the nonce.

The temple of Lugloth was a broad, squat beehive at the furthest extent of the city, its east wall abutting the city's defensive bulwark. An area had been cleared around the structure, as other religions had no wish to be too close to the noisome temple. Seanai carefully picked her way through the scattered offal and detritus festering upon the ground to approach the temple's entrance. The smooth clay lining and amorphous irregularity of the entryway was unpleasantly suggestive of any number of organic orifices. Seanai had to make a concerted effort to not cover her nose, as the draft blowing from the portal carried a fetid, charnel stench. Myriad flies swarmed to and fro and their buzzing lent a further layer of repellent horror to the structure.

"Ho, priests of Lugloth!" shouted the Ibakeen, shaking the purse of Gudea so the drakims within jingled merrily. "I come to bargain! Fourscore- That is, threescore and twenty drakims for one cadaver! A kingly price! What say you?"

Several moments passed before a figure appeared from the shadows, a short man who lurched somnambulistically from the obscene archway. He was hairless, with puffy, heavy-lidded eyes and bloated lips, his skin had an unhealthy pale bluish cast, and glistened from a coating of oil. A black robe was thrown about him haphazardly. He gave off a stench that mirrored the foul breeze blowing from inside the temple. His appearance reminded Seanai of the corpse of one who had drowned.

"For what do you wish to bargain?" he asked in a sluggish groan.

"The corpse of a girl you took two days ago. Her family will pay to have her back. There are enough drakims here to buy a similar, or even superior cadaver."

The priest cast his dull gaze upon the purse in Seanai's hand.

"Follow me."

Seanai was not enamoured with entering the temple.

"Bring the body here, to the door."

"I cannot, you must speak to our pontiff. Come."

Seanai hefted her ax suggestively.

"Be warned, priest, I am not some street slattern for you to ensnare. I have held sway over Qlgir hordes and have returned alive from the jungles of shadow haunted Iforné!"

If the recitation of Seanai's feats impressed the priest, he did not show it. He turned and receded into the building.

"Come."

Seanai was of race spawned among the grim crags of Ibak, where the unwary or dull-witted were swiftly and brutally excised. Her savage instincts screamed to her that following this man would be folly. She would find some other way to recover the girl's corpse, if she did not simply flee the city with the remainder of Gudea's drakims.

"I think not. I will inquire again later, perhaps after you have consulted with your pontiff and brought the body to-"

As Seanai spoke a swarm of figures spilled from the indecorous opening. All were reeking, hairless duplicates of the dwarfish priest who answered the door. All gripped wooden clubs in their swollen fists.

The Ibakeen dropped the purse to swing her ax with both hands, cleanly beheading the foremost attacker. But as she swung her ax back around to meet the club of the next priest, the blade broke away near the socket.

"Loins of Jhullah-Jhulku!" she cursed as she brained the priest with the ax handle.

Drawing a long Qlgir knife from her belt, she turned to flee, realizing the folly of facing the swarm of fanatics out in the open. She had not gone twenty paces when her retreat was barred by three figures. She quickly recognized one of the burnoosed men as Gudea.

"Flee, man, the priests are on my heels!"

In response, the man to Gudea's right produced a sling and hurled a missile at the Ibakeen. Catlike, she sidestepped the missile, and charged with a knife and ax haft. She cursed herself for a mooncalf, for in hindsight she felt Gudea's treachery should have been manifest.

"Swine of a costermonger! You think yourself clever? You'll brag of your guile in hell!"

Lunging, Seanai slashed the slinger across the belly with her knife, sending him to the ground clutching at his spilling entrails. Gudea retreaded, allowing his other accomplice to bear the brunt of the barbarians' fury. Seanai attempted to sidestep this man and flee into the streets beyond, but now the priests had closed the distance. They swarmed over Seanai, battering her to the ground with their clubs.

While not insensible, Seanai was stunned to immobility. She had vague awareness of being dragged roughly by her ankles across the refuse laden ground and into the temple. There followed a long, dim corridor followed by a slightly brighter chamber flickeringly lit by oil lamps. Puffy, bloated faces swam before her eyes and rough greasy hands ripped away her fine new garments. The stench of rot was overwhelming, filling her nostrils and leaving its charnel taint on throat and tongue.

Once denuded, Seanai was dragged greasily across the filthy tiles. She focused all her will on regaining her senses, as one who fights for wakefulness from an abysmal nightmare. She felt herself come to a halt, and a cold ring of metal was fastened about her right ankle, her left leg was seized and lifted, and the sound of clattering chains came to her ears. If she were to be fully shackled, she would be helpless and doomed.

Seanai struck out with fists and feet, sending her shocked captors scattering. She felt a bone break under her foot, and a shrill cry rang out. The Ibakeen opened her eyes in time to see a spear being thrust at her. With the speed of a striking viper, she writhed along the necrotically greased tiles away from the spear thrust and seized the weapon, wrenching it from the grasp of the priest who wielded it. She sprang upright and swung the spear in a wide ark, scattering her captors. With this respite gained, she took stock of her surroundings.

Lamps encircled the room, giving off noxious fumes and dull amber radiance, and some illumination filtered in from a circular skylight at the summit of the dome. The chain fettering her right leg was attached to a low, wide altar carved to resemble a pile of skulls. Three empty shackles were attached to it as well, intended to secure the limbs of anyone unfortunate enough to fall into the hands of the priests. The altar was situated in the center of a circular, dome-ceilinged chamber, its curving walls adorned with painting depicting cadaverous women besporting with varied molluscoid horrors.

Some dozen priests encircled her, lunging and probing, staying clear of her spear. Most had shed their robes and stood naked. Their pallid hides glistened oily in the lamplight. All had been crudely mutilated to remove any external indication of sex. The portions of their body that once bore these organs were now covered by angry, ruddy scar tissue. They reeked abominably and flies swarmed about them. Seanai fought the urge to retch, for a good portion of her own flesh was coated by the foul oils where the priests had handled her, and the footfalls of the innumerable flies lighting upon her skin made her shiver.

Just beyond the ring of priests stood Gudea. The sight of him filled Seanai with fury. It would be a simple matter for her to skewer him with a spearcast, but that would leave her unarmed before the priesthood. She snarled at the man.

"So, all that talk of Asirat, and the welfare of your daughter's soul was lies! What is the meaning of this treachery?"

"We approach the spring equinox, barbarian." Gudea replied serenely "It is the one time when Lugloth can manifest on the physical plane and copulate with his bride, Aghaxyl, Lady of Rot. Aghaxyl and Lugloth cannot copulate in their natural forms and must inhabit specifically prepared vessels. I offered up my daughter to house the Aghaxyl. Your arrival in Yeubedeh was fortunate, you will be a robust vessel to house Lugloth. It was simple to lure a bandit such as yourself here with promise of a reward, and Adad's surreptitious application of oil of vitriol to your ax as it rested by our door ensured its timely failure."

"Fiend! You sacrificed your daughter for this horror?"

"Nay! I spoke true when I said Shubure fell ill with fever. But it would be wasteful to burn her empty shell when it could go to serve the viscous one!"

Suddenly the room grew chill, and the light subtly altered. Gudea glanced nervously at the ceiling.

"Time grows short. We have underestimated your savagery. It seems it would have been better to have you subdued and secured upon the altar properly, now Lugloth will have to subdue you."

Seanai lunged, but the chain about her ankle drew tight. Stretching as far as she was able, she thrust at a priest who had unwisely crept too near the Ibakeen she-devil, who transfixed his thigh with the keen leaf shaped blade. Blood fountained from the split artery and the man stumbled a few yards before crumpling.

"Ha! Come closer dogs! And I'll carve you some new mutilations! You cowards would fare better to slay me from afar with spear or arrow!"

"By no means!" muttered Gudea. "While Aghaxyl can inhabit a corpse, Lugloth requires a living host,"

"Would not a man be more useful to him, and Aghaxyl?"

"The matter of the vessels sex is unimportant, save that the female body is easier for Lugloth to commandeer."

"Lugloth will find no part of this easy! I'll-"

"Best you resign yourself, barbarian! It would have gone better for you if you had allowed the priests to prepare you. You would have remained insensate as Lugloth donned your flesh as his holy garment, as it is you will know profound suffering!"

The priests became agitated, yammering and fidgeting as they stood encircling the altar. Some gesticulated toward one of the darkened portals lining the chamber. Gudea grinned broadly.

"Behold! Aghaxyl comes to embrace her lover!"

A nightmarish figure shambled into view on unsteady, spindly legs. A woman's body, now mutilated in the manner of the priests. Blackly glistening wounds marred its chest, a crudely stitched mass of pulpy flesh hung where its sex had been. Chunks of meat had been excised from the hips and buttocks. The mouth and eye sockets had been stuffed with some oozing black matter and sewn shut.

It staggered unsteadily toward the low altar, bloated and swarming with carrion insects. Waves of bilious revulsion washed over Seanai as she surmised this had been Shubure.

"Jullah Julhku!" she cursed, "You said she was dead but a day!"

Gudea nodded gravely. "The vessel must be prepared; the preparations accelerate decay."

The light in the chamber grew more otherworldly, taking on strange hues that existed on a spectrum alien to the world of men. Gudea and the priests cast their gaze to the opening in the top of the dome. Seanai seeing them thus occupied forced herself to turn her full attention to her fetters.

The manacle securing her was of rusted iron and fit tightly about her ankle as it was meant to secure smaller framed captives. It was secured by iron pins that were inserted in the hinged ends of the manacle halves. These she pried upon with the spearhead. The pins moved but slightly, and the softer metal of the spearhead gave way.

"Teats of Szongg!" she cursed and looked up to see the disposition of her tormentors. She found them enthralled by a beam of otherworldly light now focused upon the altar. Along this beam, made solid by some abyssal theurgy, crawled a sinuous mass, composed of some translucent golden starstuff. Only one end of the thing was visible, its other end disappearing out of the opening in the roof. It was thick as a man's thigh at its widest point, tapering to a fist size lump of writhing cilia at its nethermost extremity.

Seanai clamped her teeth shut upon her tongue to suppress a terrified whimper. Setting her spear aside, she crouched and seized the chain in both hands. Her feet slid alarmingly upon the slick, filth-laden tiles as she pulled upon the chain with savage fury. To her surprise, she felt the chain give slightly, and some pieces of masonry broke away where the chain was sunk into the altar. A fresh bout of wails from the priesthood drew her attention above.

The mucoid appendage penetrating the ceiling groped blindly about the altar, no doubt searching for the traditional restrained victim. Finding none, the glistening thing writhed about while emitting a high-pitched keening. As if in response, Shubure's rotting face split apart as her jaws opened impossibly wide, giving forth a low groaning exaltation that sent flies swarming wildly about her festering maw.

This spurred the priests to action, in a body, they charged at Seanai, arms and hands poised to grapple her. She disembowelled the first with a spear thrust, but the second impaled himself upon the spear, then grasped it, holding it in his body so it was torn from the Ibakeen's grip as he fell. The rest bore her to the altar and in a mass Seanai and the mutilated clergy of Lugloth fell upon the granite slab.

Seanai fought the vile clerics bitterly, lashing out with feet and fists and using the chain to batter them. The priests for their part struggled to pinion her limbs and outstretch her upon the altar for Lugloth.

Lugloth, it seemed, was not a patient god, nor an observant one. It seized a priest as an elephant's trunk might seize a tree branch. It odiously examined its howling captive with its writhing mass of cilia, and not finding its accustomed path of egress, let out an enraged squeal and smashed the priest into the altar. As if in a tantrum, Lugloth hammered the area around the altar with the unfortunate votary, pummelling two more of the faithful to bloody pulps with the ruined carcass of their brother.

Seanai narrowly avoided the same fate, only being spattered with blood and brains. Lugloth repeatedly smashed the priest's corpse into the altar with such force the granite slab began to crack. Seanai, seeing the damage to the altar, again tugged madly at the chain, calling upon the bestial gods of Ibak to strengthen her limbs.

During these proceedings, Gudea stood by dumbfounded. He was not a brave man, but he was devoted in his worship of Lugloth. Perhaps it was this piety that caused him to charge at Seanai with a club, intent on subduing her so his viscous lord might make use of her.

Seanai was nearly mad with fear and revulsion. Heedless of Lugloth's battering, she stood with legs wide braced about the ring securing the chain to the altar. She lent every iota of strength afforded her by thews forged in the grim furnace of primal barbarism to the task of wrenching the chain free. Her mind was not functioning on any conscious level, it was instinct alone that caused her to leap aside as Gudea's blow fell.

His club struck the ring and broke it free of the granite slab. Off balance from his ruined attack, Gudea stumbled and fell sprawling upon the gore spattered altar, where he was promptly seized by the coiling trunk of Lugloth. He gurgled a few curses at Seanai before he was battered into pulp. Seanai bolted from the chamber, sparing only the briefest glance at glowing golden god-slug and his carrion bride.

Outside the night was brightly lit from a point above the squat beehive of Lugloth's temple. Seanai dared not turn to gaze upon the unholy source of that illumination. As she ran, she saw the purse Gudea had given her still laying in the dust where she had dropped it. Instinctively she snatched it up.

Seanai fled the temple grounds and did not slacken her pace till she was well clear of the temple district. Presently, she leaned against the wall of a bakery, seeking her breath. She was unarmed and naked, coated in the reeking filth of Lugloth. She still tasted that foul charnel reek upon her tongue. An undeniable wave of nausea struck her and the Ibakeen retched forcefully and at length upon the cobbles of Yeubedeh.

Recovering, she spat and held up Gudea's purse, first squeezing, then shaking it. "Not much." she sneered, "barely enough drakims to hire someone to scrub this filth from me and buy a few rags to shroud my bones!"

Yeubedeh was not an active city after midnight. Looking toward the residential quarter, a wry grin spread across her face. "Gudea still owes me a dromedary." she muttered, "And I'll wager that the chest in his hall still holds enough drakims for me to outfit myself for the road ahead. Should his wife or her leering idiot of a brother seek to hinder me, all the better! I thirst for vengeance! Afterward Yeubedeh and its rotting goddess can be damned!"

THE COLOUR OF DECAY

- Ashley Dioses

Adara clung tightly to the rope with one mailed hand and scraped at the obsidian cliff with the other. The slanted, narrow ledge provided few footholds for her feet to slip into, yet she finally managed to catch them and pulled herself up and onto the precipice.

She closed her eyes, relaxed, and took in slow, deep breaths. Adara inhaled through her nose, breathing from the bottom of her lungs up until her chest expanded fully, and then exhaled through her mouth. As a hunter, she had to be strong mentally as well as physically and by meditating, she could achieve an inner quiet that would help her focus on the hunt. The Voormi, her hunting party's prey, were vile, degraded tribesmen-like creatures and they were clever. She had to be more than physically prepared to handle them for her life depended on it. Unfortunately for her, they were known to take female humans to breed with.

She visualized breathing in green light and exhaling black light, as she was taught by her former teacher. Colours were important. They represented a different energy and gave a visual indicator of what she wanted to achieve. She inhaled vitality, balance, and harmony and exhaled exhaustion, self-doubt, and hesitation. Adara imagined she was surrounded with the colour of nature itself and achieved an inner quiet.

The sun was still bright against her closed eyelids and Adara became aware of the sweat drenching her back as she lay on the ledge, the discomfort of her spear strapped on her back pressed against her armors. The heat kissed her skin, tanned from training for long hours in the sun, and scarred from past hunts. As she lay there, she realized she could hear voices; something she missed through the grunts of her companions as they continued to scale the black Eiglophian cliff.

Adara opened her eyes and got to her feet. Lord Ralibar Vooz, their leader, was nowhere to be seen. She looked back at her struggling companions but the urgency to find Ralibar was stronger. He was the High Magistrate of Commoriom and Third Cousin to King Homquat. It was her duty to protect him.

The voices she heard were softer now as they moved away and she was unable to decipher if they were from Ralibar or from Voormi. She cautiously sprinted toward the sounds, alert for anything that might impede her route. She heard shouts behind her, calling her name; she ignored them and hoped that the rest would soon follow. Adara was lean and well-built; her powerful legs allowed her to cover vast distances in a short amount of time. The terrain, however, was difficult to navigate quickly and more than once she almost slipped into furrows of lava. She had to slow her pace lest she be the one in trouble.

Ahead of her, a pillar of wispy, gray smoke rose like a gnarled claw toward the teal sky. It beckoned to her like a forest witch and her sweat became cold as it dripped down her hot skin. Slowing, Adara took out her crossbow, notched a bolt, and quietly neared the lava ridge. As she peaked over, an archaeopteryx, a night-flying scaled bird, flew just over her head, its chartreuse lizard-tail catching her full attention as it headed toward Mount Voormithadreth. The shimmering colour of its scales shone vividly against the sooty gray, dull body was distracting, and Adara almost missed Ralibar disarming himself.

Her first reaction was to shout to him yet the blankness of his expression made her pause. His eyes were unfocused, his motions were stiff and forceful, and he looked as if he were under some vile, sorcerous incantation. Goosebumps crept across her skin and time sped up as her heart pounded in her chest. She looked back down the furrow and spotted Ralibar's tormentor. An old man in ruby robes, not a Voormis, but a sorcerer, stood before a fire pit, issuing venom-filled curses at Ralibar from his cracked lips. With the speed of a sabre-tooth tiger, she aimed her crosshairs at the sorcerer, but a sudden weight fell on her arms. Adara's eyes widened and her breath caught in her throat. Her fingers became rigid at the trigger as if an invisible hand curled around her own, keeping her from releasing the bolt. Beads of sweat dripped into her emerald eyes as she tried to focus on the sorcerer. With blurry vision and a tightened grip, she could not shoot him. Adara lowered the crossbow and the weight lifted from her arms, her red hair a grimy shade of brick now plastered to her face. She wiped it from her eyes. Adara caught sight of the vivid decay-coloured tail of the bird and saw that it was leading Ralibar away.

She looked from Ralibar to the sorcerer and back. She gingerly lifted her crossbow, aimed at the sorcerer, and pulled back the bolt for the second time. Again, a strong, invisible hand gripped her own; sweat beaded down her face and into her eyes. Adara forcibly pulled her crossbow down and breathed harshly through her nose. The sorcerer was surrounded by protective magic and there was nothing she could do about it. If she failed to shoot him and he saw her, she had no doubt she would be cursed as well. She wondered if that might also be why her companions had not yet caught up to them - the whole area might be under his enchantments.

She returned her crossbow to her back and silently followed Ralibar and the archaeopteryx. The fowl led them into a maze of black stone and fallen rock, toward the pyramidal peak of Voormithadreth, which was unfamiliar to her. The echoes of her companions were suddenly clear and she wondered if they were far enough away from the sorcerer to be beyond his bewitching reach. Her companions must have taken another route to be so near and yet, out of sight. Adara froze. If she called back to them, it would alert the archaeopteryx of her presence, and it would most likely attack her. If she didn't call to them, they might never find them. Neither option appealed to her.

Adara considered the crossbow again but instead, reached for a heftier weapon. She pulled out her spear and aimed it at the foul creature. She took in a deep breath and tried to inhale a calming blue hue this time, but her imagination failed her. Black vaporous tendril shapes penetrated through her soft blue light, polluting it. A sensation of shards of ice pierced her flesh and set her very core freezing. Her spear felt like a tree limb in her hand and her arm turned to lead. The spear fell from her grip, clamouring to the ground. As soon as it left her fingers, her strength returned and the black tendrils left her mind's eye.

Adara was not surprised that the archaeopteryx was also protected by the sorcerer's magic, but the tendrils were something else entirely and made her blood run cold. They infiltrated her meditation. She stared up at the creature, keeping its lizard tail in sight, and considered upping her game. She covered the distance she lost and when she was confident she could continue to follow them through the maze, she stopped. Adara sat down cross-legged and placed her hands on her knees. She straightened her spine, closed her eyes, and took in slow, deliberate breaths.

Instead of inhaling a select colour this time, she visualized an iridescent hue emanating from the crown of her head and flowing down through her body until it surrounded her like a bubble. The shield she created for herself was a force of shimmering cracked mirrors. Any geas or spell directed at her would be reflected back. And anything seeking her out, with tendrils or otherwise, would only see themselves. She would be invisible to outside magical forces.

The Huntress stood as tall as any man in Ralibar's hunting party and was ranked among the best hunters in Commoriom. So when the High Magistrate of Commoriom and Third Cousin to King Homquat, Lord Ralibar Vooz, asked her to join in on a hunt for Voormi on the slopes of the black Eiglophian Mountains, Adara did not hesitate to accept his invitation. Her father had trained her since she was a child to be the best hunter she could be. He had no concerns that he only had a daughter, and not a son, to teach his trade to. Others were not so accepting but she did not care. The only person she had to prove her capabilities to was the king himself. She worked hard and trained long in every skill that could possibly be of use in hunting game. Alongside the normal physical tests of the hunt, she developed a great mental strength which allowed her to excel at meditation and free herself from distractions.

Not surprisingly, Adara was eager to be schooled in advanced meditations when she was older-at six-and-twenty years of age-which singled her out. Her fellow hunters cared only to meditate as much as the hunt required, which was to say, only for clearing their heads in order to be observant to clues from their preys' trail. Ralibar was sceptical of magic, yet Adara knew she could potentially be up against such threats, especially in these unknown territories, where ancient gods were rumoured to reside. She, however, was unsure how she felt about actually needing to use her shielding techniques for they had been untested until now.

Adara opened her eyes and continued to follow Ralibar and the night-flying bird through the labyrinth. As she followed them, she thought back to the tendrils. The more she pictured them in her head, the less like tendrils she thought they were. Two appeared at first and they were wispy and dark. Yet, as more entered her vision, the more she thought the tendrils were rigid rather than fluid. They appeared jointed rather than smooth.

The archaeopteryx led them to a series of cavern-mouths at the upper mountain and soared toward the lowest one. Adara immediately regretted not waiting for her companions as she saw the Voormi swarm out of the caverns. Her shielding only worked against magical attacks, not physical ones. Roughly made weapons such as sharpened bones and stones were thrown at Ralibar, who was able to escape serious injury from the small protection the archaeopteryx lent. Adara, however, could not stay hidden if she wanted to continue following Ralibar. There was no way to get passed the Voormi without being seen.

The archaeopteryx began attacking those Voormi who neared Ralibar and Adara took the chance to fire bolts at them in quick succession. As soon as she was discovered, they rushed her. She dodged various garbage projectiles and pulled out her spear. Trekking the terrain through the labyrinth gave her enough familiarity to navigate her footing well enough, but this was the Voormi's home. Still, she was able to take out many of them before she was finally overcome.

Adara's spear was wretched away and broken in two, her crossbow and daggers were tossed aside. She felt teeth and claws hit against the links on her armour until it was also ripped away, leaving her in only her jerkin. She delivered blow after blow with her mailed fists until a swift rock to her head almost knocked her out. Adara was then lifted up like a doll, impressive for she was nearly twice their height, and carried to one of the caverns. Her emerald eyes, open to slits, blurred in the shade of the cavern, yet she still saw that they were heading into a different one than the one Ralibar entered. She groaned and reached out to try to grab part of the cavern wall but her fingers just grazed the rock sides.

Though the Voormi were short, they barely reached her midriff, they were abnormally strong, allowing them to carry her without a problem. Their canine-like yells sounded eerily like victorious, sinister, hoorahs as they echoed through the narrow pathway. The Huntress held on to consciousness as long as she could. Wetness streamed down her face and she hoped it was just sweat. She willed herself to keep her eyes open, even in the darkness, to gauge where she was headed. The path kept going straight, then descended steeply. They continued some ways and then turned left into a room. Adara was lifted off the shoulders of a Voormis and thrown onto a thin pile of straw. The force of the throw reverberated through her skull and then she saw black.

Something began to crack. Slightly, at first, and then a great crash echoed through Adara's mind. Something like glass shattered into thousands of pieces. The tendril-like members did not return but instead, a pattern of thread weaved throughout her mind in iridescent colours of green. Glimmers of smaragdine, emerald, lime, and chartreuse flickered against a sooty background. As she peered closer between the pattern, she thought she could see movement. Something not quite as black, perhaps charcoal, hid in the background.

A sudden spike of pain shot through her head, breaking the vision, and waking her up. A Voormis pressed his knee against her head to hold her down while he focused intently on removing her jerkin. Her head throbbed immensely as he pressed right against her injury. Adara grunted as she tried to lift his knee off but he had her at a disadvantage. He issued a noise that sounded closely like laughter and Adara worked furiously against his weight. Her mailed gloves had been taken as well as her shoes, but her belt remained.

With any luck, she should still have one of her small throwing darts. The daggers she carried were too big and were easily seen and taken away. Adara, however, also carried small, concealable darts in case she was in tight situations. With one fist pounding into his knee, which for anyone else would have broken it, Adara reached for her belt with the other, just as the Voormis was unbuckling it. He pressed down harder, making

Adara gasp. Black spots entered her vision but she managed to grip one of her darts and drive it through his knee. He howled in agony and then, with his full body weight, drove his elbow into her stomach. Adara yelled out but managed to recover enough to block her face from being smashed in by a makeshift club. The Voormis put his whole body into the swing, and when the club hit the floor, Adara rolled back and wrapped her legs around his neck. She forced the arm holding the club back at an angle and squeezed her thighs. The Voormis struggled for air, blank eyes rolled to the back of his head as he beat futilely against her thighs, until finally he slumped over. Adara loosened her hold, kicking the body hard across the room, into the cave wall.

Her head was spinning and her body ached. Blood left her hair, temple, and cheeks sticky and she hoped it was all just from his knee wound. She gingerly touched her head and felt an open gash from where the rock was originally smashed, about the length of her thumb and narrow. Nothing too big, but it kept bleeding and she needed to wrap it quickly. Adara ripped part of her jerkin and wrapped the wound as best she could. She re-tied her messy, red hair so it was out of her face and away from the wound. There was nothing she could do about the pain and she knew time was running out. She had no idea how long she was out for, or where Ralibar was. Other Voormi would be coming to see what the noises were, and she did not want to stay for that.

Adara put her belt back on and replaced her dart. She opened the rough gate made of sticks that led back to the main pathway and listened. She could hear canine howls from her right and quickly turned left. Her bruised midsection throbbed every time she took deep breaths and every step yielded sharp jabs from the bones and rocks under her bare feet. The air grew thicker the lower she descended and she became disoriented.

The darkness finally began to brighten by a hidden glow and the pathway opened up to an underground hall. Adara only stopped to rest by plopping down on the cold, hard ground when she was sure she couldn't hear the Voormi behind her anymore. Sweat trailed down her skin and her chest heaved. She leaned against the wall and tried to focus on the source of the glowing light but could not determine where it was coming from.

She thought about her vision and realized that the cracking glass she heard was her shield breaking. The mirror she projected to protect herself had shattered. That was impossible though, the cracked mirror projection should have reflected any magic back to the sender. Yet it penetrated again and entered her dream. Only Supreme Divine magic could do that, or so she was led to believe by her teachers.

She shook her head and immediately regretted it. Magic from a divine being would have no problem breaking through anything she conjured up. But to have that happen to begin with meant that she attracted the attention from such a being and though some are reputed to live there, that seemed highly unlikely. What made her so special as to gain the gaze of something divine? Surely an escaped prisoner of Voormi did not garner such attention. Maybe it wasn't Supreme Divine magic breaking through her shield at all. Maybe she just dreamed her shield wasn't holding up as it should. It was something she'd never had to do on the hunt before. Even during practice, she really didn't have anything to practice against. Shielding against sorcery, let alone Supreme Divine magic, was not something one could accurately practice against without the actual threat.

Adara relaxed a little. She was thinking too much and her head wound wasn't helping. The iridescent greens and the patterns against a sooty backdrop resembled to her now, the yellow-green scales of the archaeopteryx against its soot-coloured body. It made sense. The night-flying creature was stuck on her mind. If only she could catch sight of that colourful tail, she could find Ralibar.

She had to take care of herself first though. She thought back to her training and recalled a healing meditation. It was not difficult to close her eyes, as they were already heavy, but Adara was determined to heal herself and not give way to sleep. The Voormi could easily take this pathway and discover her if they were persistent enough. She straightened her spine, with the help of the wall, and placed her bloody hands lightly on her knees, barely noticing the pain emanating from her raw knuckles. Her head sent a rainbow of flashing colours through her mind as the gash continued to ache, but Adara ignored it, and focused on green light again. She inhaled the colour of healing through her nose and exhaled black. She imagined green light coming through her crown and travelling down her spine, healing everything in its wake. She imagined that several times, until her stomach stopped aching and her head pain was reduced to a dull throb.

Once she was sure she had enough strength to continue on, Adara stood up, though still somewhat shakily. The path past the hall became narrower and lower than the pathway the Voormi travelled on and she had to crouch to make it through. The path was heavily covered in jagged rocks, which made it difficult to traverse with her bare feet. The dim, unnatural light cast her shadow in several directions and made it harder for her to see if anything else was moving through the cave with her. A ringing in her ears also made it hard for her to detect soft sounds made from light footsteps. Thick, dusty cobwebs began to impede her journey and she became confident that she was alone. The path must not have been frequented underneath this part of Voormithadreth.

Adara considered what options she had left. She had no armour, no shoes, and carried a few small throwing darts that remained hidden inside her belt. The archaeopteryx had already proved itself invulnerable to her weapons and there were too many Voormi to fight off again. Though she was able to travel, she was still not entirely healed and definitely not in any prime condition to fight.

One option was to find a way out of the mountain and locate the rest of her hunting party. There, she could regroup and hunt together to find Ralibar. On the other hand, if she left and headed back, she might never have a chance of finding him before the geas finished its course. Ralibar needed her, and she was closer than anyone else in helping him, despite what little help she could give. She decided that she would choke Ralibar out as quickly and quietly as she could, drag him to one of the hidden pathways, and hope the archaeopteryx didn't notice. The archaeopteryx, being primarily nocturnal, would make it a difficult plan to execute, but Adara hoped that it would not know every hidden pathway in the vicinity.

The pathway began to widen and eventually led to the mouth of a cave. The air grew acrid and metallic-tasting and Adara wondered if her own blood was strengthening the pungent odour. She ripped off more of her jerkin and wrapped her bleeding feet. If she kept descending into the mountain by using forgotten pathways, the terrain would continue to get rougher. She also didn't want to leave a blood trail for Voormi or anything else to track.

As Adara began wrapping her second foot, movement in the cave ahead of her caught her attention. She froze and stared past the cave mouth. Her shadows halted and the dim glow cast no other moving shadows within the pathway. She waited and saw it again... a glimmer of green.

Adara hastily finished wrapping her foot and hurried quietly to the entrance of the cave mouth. A great chasm loomed before her, and beyond it, within the darkness, shone various shades of green. Amongst them, the flickering of chartreuse teased her. It had to have been the archaeopteryx flying above, and yet, Ralibar should have been following close behind, but on what? She searched around the chasm to find a bridge, but only saw sooty strands of thread. They formed intricate patterns across the chasm, a type of bridge, then?

Being lighter than Ralibar, though not by much, Adara moved swiftly, and confidently over the strands toward the flickering chartreuse tail. Her mouth curved into a smirk as she neared it, but it was instantly gone as her foot caught on something, and she dropped to a knee. The strand dangerously wobbled from side to side, threatening to throw her off and into the depths below. Once able to steady herself, she looked behind her to see what had impeded her movements. Her hastily wrapped foot had unravelled and was sticking to the strand beneath her. Adara reached out to pull herself up and found another strand in the darkness to grab onto. As she pulled herself up, something crashed onto the strand ahead - it was a sizeable dead bird, stricken with decay and wrapped in many dark, silky strands.

Adara's heart jumped into her mouth as she realized this was the chartreuse glimmer she had seen. She looked around and saw that the other various green glimmers were other prey in different stages of decay. They were all wrapped in the same thread she was standing on and now, she realized why the dead were moving. She had abandoned her hunter's instinct and recklessly raced after her so-called prey without assessing her surroundings. Now she knew she had become the hunted. Many pelts decorated her floors, and select heads graced her walls at home, but she vowed she would never become a trophy, to suitors or otherwise. Though a highly skilled hunter, she was not a warrior and her training in meditation was a far cry from the powers of a sorceress.

Adara was wise enough to realize she was not the hunter anymore. She spun around and attempted to race back the way she had come, but her way was blocked. Standing before Adara was the penetrator of her visions, and the weaver of her dreams. Her body was as big as a crouching woman, but the great length of her legs reached out wide. The tendril-like black vapours that entered Adara's vision were jointed, ebony legs. The cracking of her mirrored shield crumpled against the spider-god's fangs, and the chartreuse flickering of the dead prey masked her sooty web as the Spider-God, Atlach-Nacha lured her prey.

"You are not covered in metal shards," the Spider-God whispered.

Adara pulled out the darts from her belt, and threw them

with swift, precise aim, but they amounted to nothing, merely bouncing off the great spider's body to drop into the underworld sea below. Adara watched helplessly as they fell away then met Atlach-Nacha's gaze of many black, beady eyes. Adara had no choice, but to stand, as something fast and sharp stabbed her through her stomach. She gasped and felt the venom flow through her, bringing numbness with it. Fresh, steaming blood trailed down her torso and legs.

The Huntress kept her gaze fixated on the spider-god as she attempted to take deep breaths. This time, Adara visualized gold light flowing from her crown, down her spine, and to the soles of her feet. She imagined its warmth coursing through her bones and muscles. She imagined it was healing her stomach wound and fighting back the toxins. She visualized this quickly, over and over again, until her breathing became laboured, and her concentration was lost.

"It would have been burdensome to extract those metal shards from your friend, so I decided to let him go. You, I could see, when you entered your daydreams. I could see when you lost your metal shards. I am grateful that you came," Atlach-Nacha whispered. The spider-god wrapped the Huntress up tenderly, lovingly. Before Adara finally closed her eyes, she saw that Atlach-Nacha had placed her amongst the decaying, chartreuse-coloured prey...

THE LUCKY THIEF

- Tim Mendees

The city gate clanged shut behind the master thief as he stumbled towards the well. Night had fallen and the twin pink moons cast the courtyard in long shadows that hid a hundred pairs of inquisitive eyes. Overhead, two shantaks wheeled north, heading for the mountains. The monstrous winged beasts appeared locked in a dance that could have been either courtship or combat. Rivvens paid them little attention as he raised the bucket, dipped his water-skein into the fragrant liquid and slaked his thirst.

He'd been on the road for what felt like an eternity. The only thing that ached more than his feet was his head. Sobriety wasn't something he was accustomed to enduring. It had been days since he'd last had even a sniff of ale, the long slog from the last town made even more arduous by some thieving scoundrel making off with his supplies as he'd slept off a skin-full in an abandoned barn. Oh, the irony. That was usually his trick. How he'd survived crossing the Jungle of Parg with a single skein of water was something of a mystery, and spoke of the motivation of avarice.

As Rivvens dipped his drinking vessel back into the bucket for a refill, something warm and comforting rubbed against his leg, vibrating in time with its breathing.

"Ah, 'ello, Puss, good to see ye again. I 'aven't got that fishy I promised ye yet, I'll see about sortin' it out once I've been paid."

The cat looked at him askew.

"Ye 'aven't seen a whoreson answering to the name o' Geifermann, 'ave ye?"

The cat cocked his head, then wandered lazily in the direction of *The Cotter's Lament*, one of Ulthar's rowdiest drinking establishments.

Rivvens smiled. "Figures ye'd be back 'ere, ye old lush." His contact, a fence and black marketeer by the name of Geifermann had failed to meet him at their pre-arranged rendezvous in Dylath-Leen. Since then, he'd been in every low-down drinking pit in the Western Dreamlands.

Knocking the worst of the dust from his cloak, Rivvens followed the portly tabby towards the Inn, mentally inventing creative penalties to inflict on Geifermann should he not have his coin as arranged. The cat stopped by the door and rolled on his back for a belly rub. Rivvens, despite his knees and back screaming, crouched and obliged. After all, it wasn't wise to get on the wrong side of the feline rulers of Ulthar.

"Thanks, Puss," he grimaced, straightening, and pulling the door ajar. A miasma of pipe smoke and stale alcohol met him as he stepped inside. It was as welcome as a kiss from a Celephaïs courtesan after what he had endured since he set out on Geifermann's *little job*.

Pausing just inside, he carefully studied the patrons to ensure he wasn't about to run into any trouble. A man in his line of work has a habit of making enemies, it always paid to be cautious. The inn was full of the worst kind of bandit and mercenary imaginable. It didn't look like there was an honest man amongst them. This was good. He was as safe here as anywhere. A thief-taker would have been spotted instantly and turned into cat food before you could say *Nyarlathotep*.

As Rivvens looked for his quarry, his attention was drawn to the far end of the bar by a familiar chuckle. Skirting a table of ghouls playing a round of bones, he peered around the wooden beam that had obscured the table from view. "There ye are... ye bulbous bastard."

Geifermann poured out a couple of coins into his pudgy mitt and passed them to the barkeep. The hulking fellow took the payment and slammed a foaming tankard down in front of his customer. "Cheers!" Geifermann beamed, his cheeks rosy and his ginger beard bristling. He was about to tip his head back and take a swig when...

Thump!

An iron sword slammed down on the table next to him.

"Hey, watch it, ye big hairy lump, ye nearly spilled me ale slammin' yer sword down like that!"

Stepping into the candlelight, Rivvens lowered his hood and flashed a predatory grin.

"Oh, It's ye!" Geifermann held out a clammy fist in greeting. "Upon me soul, Rivvens, what brings ye back to this festering hole?"

Rivvens slapped his contact's hand aside. "Ye know full well what I'm doing here, ye old weasel. I've been looking fer ye in every cess-pool from Dylath-Leen to Galmez. Anyone would think that ye didn't want to be found, am I right?"

"Yes... well... I've had to lay low. There was some

unpleasantness in Taren." Geifermann looked furtively around the inn before taking a swig of ale.

"Ha!" Rivvens erupted into a fit of mirth. "I 'eard. Something about defective chastity belts, wasn't it?"

Geifermann choked and spluttered as his ale went down the wrong hole. Once he had composed himself, he held a stubby finger to his lips. "Hush! Ye don't know who's listenin'."

"Yeah, any one of these clodhoppers could be in the employ of the convent... heh!"

"No need to take the proverbial, Rivvens. Those holy terrors have put a damn price on me head."

"Ha, I know, I 'eard. It's delicious," Rivvens paused to make a show of looking around. "Well, I don't think ye get many of the sisterhood in a rats-nest like this, I think yer safe... fer the time being."

"I am if ye keep yer big trap shut!" Geifermann held up a hand, it was trembling visibly. "Dammit, look what ye've done now. Me 'ands are shakin' again... It's taken six hours of solid drinkin' to steady 'em... Fancy one?"

"Aye. Make it large and make it strong."

"Marvellous," Geifermann lifted his ale to his lips and drained his tankard in three mighty gulps. Even Rivvens was impressed. "Innkeep, two more of *these*, if you'd be so kind?"

The barkeep grunted and filled two tankards, plonking them down in front of Rivvens and Geifermann with all the delicacy of a zoog in a hen-house. Snatching Geifermann's coins from the table, he stalked away to menace his next customer.

Rivvens grabbed his tankard firmly by the bone and silver handle and poured a third of it down his gullet. "Ruddy 'ell," he spluttered, showering his friend with spittle. "That stuff will put hairs on yer chest... No wonder yer nose is as red as a blasted beetroot."

"Well, it's medicinal, ain't it? Being chased all over the Garden Lands by a bunch of zealots waving flaming pitchforks gives ye one hell of a thirst, let me tell ye."

"Ha, I can well imagine, old chum... Anyway, as delightful as it is revelling in yer misfortune, we have a little bit of *business* to take care of."

"Ye mean?" Geifermann's eyes started to twinkle like two diamonds poking out of a compost heap.

"Aye, I got it. No thanks to yer blasted map!"

Geifermann's cheeks flushed an even deeper shade of red. "Hey... err... I don't know what ye..."

"Cut the crap, Geef. Ye know damn well, that map was about as much use as a eunuch in a whorehouse!"

"Hey," Geifermann did his best to look both innocent and affronted. "I'll have ye know, I got that map in good faith from one of the ghouls that live out near Khem."

Rivvens sighed. "Aye, And I'll wager it was the same dog-faced scoundrel that ye got yer wonky lockable bloomers from, am I right?"

"Well... um..."

"I knew it!" Rivvens levelled a finger between Geifermann's eyes. "When are ye goin' to learn that nothin' good comes from tradin' with those damn corpse-eaters in the desert?"

Geifermann shrugged. "But, ye got the stone?"

"Aye... I got the blasted stone alright." Rivvens took another slurp of ale and wiped his mouth on the back of one of his moon-beast-hide gloves."

"But, how, if the map was useless?" Geifermann cocked a bushy ginger eyebrow.

"That, my friend, is a rather long story, ye'd better get another round in... I'll need something to steady me nerves."

Geifermann sighed and pulled his coin purse from inside his grubby tunic. "Fine... Innkeep, another two, if ye please."

The barkeep loomed over the table, blocking out all light save that from the guttering candle between them. "'You got the coin?"

Geifermann grinned and jangled his purse. "Aye, I'm good fer it."

Grunting and snatching up the tankards, the barkeep marched back behind the bar, and then returned with two refills. Geifermann grinned from ear to ear as he made a show of depositing each coin in the man's hand. It felt good to have coin for a change. Muttering oaths and casting aspersions on Geifermann's lineage, the Barkeep wandered off to do a sweep for empties.

"So, come on, then, Rivvens. How in Leng did ye manage to find the stone if the map was as worthless as ye say?"

"Well, I left the tavern in high spirits..."

"That's one word fer it, ye were well tiddly."

"Are ye goin' to shut yer flap an' let me tell the story, or what?"

"Sorry, Rivvens, go on."

Rivvens took a slurp to wet his whistle. "Anyway, I stroked the old tabby outside the Inn fer a bit of luck, then followed the road west into the Enchanted Wood...

* * *

It was a balmy night as Rivvens weaved through the Ulthar city gate and took the winding path into the woods. The air was heady with the scent of wet leaves and night blossoms calming his spirit and luring him into a languid state. Pausing by a clump of brightly-coloured fungi, he took the map that Geifermann had given him from his knapsack and unfurled it. Its providence was obvious to his experienced eye, the scratchy illustration had been created using a charred bone... the calling card of the ghouls.

"Dammit, Geef, this is about as easy to follow as shoggoth poetry."

Scratching his stubbly chin, he searched the undergrowth for a path leading north-west. There wasn't one. There was, however, one leading north and one leading west. He took the northern path and hoped for the best. According to the map, he should have followed it for around a quarter of a mile then veered east. Unfortunately, after less than a hundred yards, his progress was blocked by a wall of six-foot glowing thistles. Rivvens drew his trusty short sword and hacked a couple of them down. Peering through his newly-created gap, he realised that the spiky triffids stretched on for some considerable distance. He wasn't going that way.

"Damn it all to Leng, I'll 'ave to retrace me steps."

This is what he did, and soon he was back at the edge of the wood peering at the Ulthar gate in the distance. "I 'ave a good mind to march back in there and shove this pile of shantak dropping up yer flabby backside, Geef."

Rivvens took one of the several skeins he had filled with wine from his belt and took a mouthful. Once done, he held the vessel up to the moonlight and shrugged. "Maybe it's the booze.

I'll give it another go before I decide to go back and give him a good slap." His explanation would have made sense had Rivvens not been travelling the dreamlands on a belly-full of booze since he was a whelp. Still, it always paid to double check.

This time, when he reached the branching point, Rivvens took the western path instead. "This looks more like it," he mumbled as the path snaked deeper into the wood. A gentle breeze tossed the foliage to and fro in an oddly hypnotic dance as he pressed on through ancient yew trees smothered in moss and ivy. The violet light from the moons coming through the branches created a dizzying mosaic on the forest floor.

Rivvens started to relax and checked the map once more. Soon, he should encounter a clearing with a tree that had been struck by lightning in the centre. As landmarks go, this one would be tricky to miss. However, after another ten minutes of walking, all Rivvens had found were healthy yew trees.

"Stupid map... I'm startin' to think that all this is good for is wiping my backside on," he paused and squinted through the trees and bushes. Over to his left, something caught his eye. It looked like an old wood-cutter or poacher's shack. He checked the map again. There was a shack depicted, but it was on the far side of the wood. Nowhere near his current position.

He'd been walking for close to two hours by this point and deemed it prudent to investigate the shack as a potential shelter for the night. All the drink and the soft violet light were making his eyelids droop. Even if the shack was inhabited, he may be able to ask for directions to the lightning tree. It was said to house one of the gates to upper slumber, so how hard could it be to find? His approach was hard to gauge, should he sneak up and risk startling any friendly occupant, or blunder across whistling a jaunty tune and risk being set upon by bandits, crazies... or worse? In the end, he chose the former.

Carefully picking his way towards the shack, Rivvens moved quickly and quietly. Even in his inebriated state, the experienced thief moved like a phantom, avoiding every twig and clump of vegetation. Nearing the shack, he crouched behind the twisted trunk of a yew tree and produced his spyglass from the pouch on his belt.

"Hmm, no signs o' life." In fact, the shack looked like it had been vacant for quite some time. It was close to falling down, teetering precariously to the left. Diseased-looking mushrooms sprouted from leprous clumps of fungi around the base and the walls were thick with black mould. Still, it would be better, and safer, than sleeping out on the road. The enchanted wood was home to several predatory species - and that just counted the humanoid ones.

Replacing his spyglass and drawing his short sword, Rivvens stalked closer, the stench of decay filling his nostrils. Using the creak of overhead branches to mask his opening of the door, he let it drift slowly ajar and listened for any movement. When he was sure it was deserted, he stepped into the gloom and looked for a candle or lamp. An old rickety table next to the door proved to have both a candle stub and a box of *Cthugha's Fury* matches. Rivvens struck one and lit the wick.

"What in Nodens' name?" Apart from the table and a rickety chair, the only furniture was a mouldering bed. It wasn't any of these that had made him gasp, however. What had startled him was the far wall. Constructed of random pieces of wood secured at strange angles then inlaid with slivers of mirror-glass, the wall resembled a vortex.

Rivvens left the lamp burning, left the shack and went around to the rear. "Eh?" He scratched his head in confusion. It was just an ordinary wooden wall. Moving closer, he gingerly put his hand on it then jerked it away upon feeling a faint vibration.

"That's it... I'm outta here," deciding that there was no shame in fearing the unknown, Rivvens decided to steal the lamp and leave. Hurrying around to the door, he stepped inside once more and instantly stood slack-jawed.

The wall was starting to rotate.

"How can this be?"

"Tee-hee!" A squeaky voice called out. "Now you're in trouble... she's coming home!"

"What? ... Who... where are you?"

"She's... gonna... get you!"

Rivvens drew his sword, waving it at the darkened corners. "Show yourself!"

"Here she comes..."

The wall glistened with shimmering light then started to ripple and undulate, finally dissolving to reveal another room beyond. It was unlike any room he'd seen before. It was long and cramped with a sloping ceiling. In the far corner, next to a desk overflowing with books, was a brass-framed bed with a sleeping man on it. At the foot of the bed, a bent old crone loomed over the sleeper, a screaming baby dangling by its foot from one hand and a wavy ceremonial dagger in the other.

Rivvens had seen enough. He knew a witch when he saw one. They weren't the most welcoming of people at the best of times, especially if they were in the middle of *something.* Deciding that his only hope of survival was to remain unseen, he blew out the lamp and started to creep towards the door. His fingers closed around the handle just as something leapt onto the table and nearly made him scream.

"Auntie Kesiah will gut you if she finds you in her shack," the squeaky voice belonged to a plump brown rat with a human face and hands.

"So shut up an' let me go then," Rivvens whispered, pulling the door open.

"Ah, ah... No, no," the rat tittered. "All it would take is one squeak."

"Don't squeak then."

"What's in it for me?"

Rivvens sighed. He'd met familiars before... they were always on the make. "What do ye want, ye little swindler?"

"Now, now, no need to be rude. Let's see, hmm," he pointed to his knapsack. "What's in there?"

"I have coin if ye want it?"

"What the buggery would I need coin for? I'm a bloody rat!"

"Fine," Rivvens had a rummage. The last thing he wanted to do was part with any provisions, but he didn't have much choice. "How about a lump of cheese?"

"You got yourself a deal."

Rivvens plonked the lump down on the table and stepped out of the door. As soon as his feet hit the soil, the rat started to shriek. "Auntie Kesiah, Auntie Kesiah, a man is in your shack!"

"You little..." Rivvens stopped himself from returning, sword in hand, as a clap like thunder echoed from within. Foregoing the sweet pleasure of revenge, he instead took off at a breakneck pace through the trees.

His heart pounding like crazy, Rivvens leapt over fallen tree limbs and through scratchy shrubs that snagged at his garments and tore any exposed flesh. He didn't dare look if the witch was in pursuit. His only thought was to get as far away from the shack as quickly as he possibly could. He ran until his lungs burned and he couldn't run a single step further. Collapsing to the ground at the base of a towering oak, he lay on his back and sucked in air.

Minutes passed before his blurred vision returned to normal and his blood stopped roaring in his ears. "...bastard," he sighed, finally able to finish the sentence he'd started back at the shack. "I should 'ave known not to trust a bloody familiar." Sitting up, he looked around and sighed. "Great... Now I really am lost. Geef, if I ever find my way back to town, I'm gonna bloody kill ye."

Dragging himself backwards, Rivvens propped himself up against the gnarled trunk and unhooked one of his skeins. After chugging back a good few mouthfuls of the potent wine, he started to chuckle to himself. The situation was ridiculous. He'd crossed the Enchanted Wood a thousand times and never once become lost. The funniest thing about it was, if he hadn't followed Geifermann's wretched map, and had instead followed his own instincts, he would at least be somewhere he knew. As it stood, he didn't have a clue about his whereabouts. All sense of location and direction had become lost during his panicked flight.

The dense canopy in this section of the wood cut the moonlight down to a dim glow that didn't reach the floor. Despite the lack of light and his recent encounter with a hag, Rivvens felt relaxed. So much so, that his eyelids started to droop. Instead of fighting off the urge for slumber, he made a conscious choice to catch forty winks and attempt to navigate himself back to civilisation come daybreak. Within seconds, he was drifting off.

It couldn't have been longer than five minutes before he was startled awake by a furtive rustle from a bush to his right. Quick as a flash, Rivvens was on his feet, steadying himself with one hand on the oak and drawing his blade with the other. He was visibly swaying due to the alcohol but did his best to look formidable.

"Hello? Show yerself, damn you!"

Another rustle drew his attention over two the left. He turned to face it, his mind racing. Was it the witch? Was it one of the footpads or highwaymen that used the woods as a hunting ground? Was it something worse? Something *unspeakable.* His questions were soon answered as his stalker broke cover...

"Damn... bloody zoogs, that's all I need."

The furry menace was around the size of a well-fed cat and covered in mangy orange fur. It had bat-like ears and globular unblinking eyes similar to those of an owl. The creature's muzzle was tipped with several thrashing tentacles that tasted the air like serpents and waved hungrily in his direction.

"Keep back, ye little bugger," Rivvens positioned the blade in a defensive manner, ready to fend off a leaping attack. He'd dealt with zoogs before. The little predators used their speed and acrobatic ability to go straight for the jugular. Still, he wasn't concerned. One hungry zoog wasn't much of a threat...

Rustle.

"Oh bugger!" His heart sank as several more zoogs, some larger than the first, started to peek out from under the bushes surrounding the tree. This wasn't good. In his drunken state, he'd failed to notice the burrows and tell-tale scratches on the tree. Rivvens had blundered into a nest.

"Keep back."

Sensing his mounting fear, the first zoog chittered in amusement before springing forward like a furry cannonball. Rivvens ducked aside and caught it with a glancing blow with the hilt of his sword. The zoog spun off into the foliage, hissing and spitting in fury. He didn't have time to savour his victory, however, as two more zoogs mounted an attack, one from the ground, one from the branches above.

Rivvens booted the first one with such force that it was sent airborne, the second dropped onto his back and dug its claws into his skin. Grunting with pain, Rivvens leapt backwards, sandwiching the zoog between himself and the tree. It fell from his body and squirmed at his feet. As he positioned his blade to deliver a cleaving strike to the beast's neck, the bushes started to shake and rustle as reinforcements arrived.

His heart missing several beats, Rivvens spared the zoog and bolted through the trees. For the second time that night, he found himself crashing blindly through the woods. This time, in contrast to the first, he knew damn well that he was being chased. Zoogs whooped and chittered as they tore through the undergrowth and leapt from branch to branch.

As he raced for his life, Rivvens suddenly realised that he had left his knapsack, together with all of its contents, some crucial to the mission, under the tree. He paused for a second and looked back the way he had come. Should he try and go back to retrieve it?

"Bugger that," he decided upon seeing upward of twenty zoogs scampering along the ground towards him. Letting out a yelp of fear, he resumed running.

Fuzzy-headed from all the ale and wine, coupled with the exertion, left Rivvens feeling quite nauseated. He was so busy sucking in air and trying not to vomit that he didn't notice a large log lying across the trail. His right boot connected, sending him tumbling head over heels through a bush and down a slope. Rivvens plummeted down the bank for what seemed like days, finally hitting the bottom with a mighty *thud.* The back of his head struck a jagged rock protruding from the soil...

Everything went black...

* * *

Rivvens took a slurp of ale. "When I came to, I was staring up at a circle of peddlers with beards like rose bushes. Seriously, Geef, I've never seen face-fungus like it, ye could have thatched a roof with the fallout."

Geifermann chuckled. "Was it one of the caravans?"

"Aye, they were heading from Dylath-Leen to Sinara when they found me."

"That was bloody lucky, then. The chances of bumping into one of those is slimmer than that tavern wench over by the door. How come the zoogs didn't attack them? Numbers?"

Rivvens shook his head. "Nah, cats... They had a litter of Ulthar's finest guarding the convoy. Obviously old hands at crossing the wood. They helped me up and gave me some wine, which was very welcome, I can tell ye. It banished me hangover in a couple of sips. Me 'ead was still throbbing though, I had a mighty duck egg on the back of me noggin. One of the old peddler women saw to it and stitched up the gash. She did a damn good job of it too... look."

Leaning over the table, Geifermann took a look at the scar and whistled appreciatively. "I'm impressed. She could sew finery fer the damn Duke with needlework skills like that." He brought his tankard to his lips and imbibed.

"Indeed. It was her who told me that I was lookin' in the wrong place fer the temple."

For the second time that evening, Geifermann nearly choked on his ale. When he was done spluttering, he wagged a finger at Rivvens. "What the hell did ye tell her fer? Don't the words *secret mission* mean anything to ye?"

"Come off it, Geef, that map wasn't fit to wipe me arse with. I needed directions if I was going to lay me hands on that damned stone... anyway, I'd lost the map."

"What?" Geifermann buried his face in his palm. "That map cost me an arm an' a leg... literally. I nearly broke me back exhuming that noblewoman's corpse. Trading with ghouls is 'ard work."

Rivvens shrugged. "Yeah, well, I lost the map, me supplies... everything. I'd left me knapsack behind when I fled the zoogs. I'd even lost those fancy black gloves ye gave me."

Geifermann turned pale. "What? Ye lost the gloves, then... Oh, you didn't..." he trailed off, biting his lip.

"What? I didn't what?"

"Oh... nothing."

Rivvens slammed his fist down on the table making their tankards hop a couple of inches. "Spit it out, ye moon-beast's rump!"

"Hey, hey," Geifermann held up his hands, "it's nothing, honest. I just liked those gloves, is all." He took another swig of ale. "Anyway, It was the old hag that patched ye up who told ye how to find the temple of Tsathoggua?"

"Aye, she'd stumbled across it as a child when her father's caravan fled a bandit attack. They were good enough to give me a ride on the cart with all the moggies as far as the Yann border then sent me on me way. Before I left them, I bought more supplies and she sketched a map fer me."

"The old crone sketched ye a map?"

Rivvens smirked. "Aye, and it was a damn sight more useful than the one ye gave me."

Geifermann rolled his eyes. "Shut up about the ruddy map, already, Rivvens. It wasn't my blasted fault, I traded the finest blue-blood carrion fer that map. Bloody ghoul, I'll skin his scabrous hide next time I see him."

"It wasn't one of the Pickman clan, was it? Bastards to a beast, that rotten lot."

"Nah, It was one of the Carters... Anyway, tell me about the temple."

Rivvens drained his tankard. "Aye, right, I'll tell ye in a minute. Get another round in, I'm off to drain the mire-beast." With that, he stood and weaved through the tables towards the door at the rear of the inn.

"Innkeep! Two more, if ye would be so kind?"

The barkeeper scowled at Geifermann and grunted in the affirmative. Moments later, he returned with two fresh tankards, plonked them down, took the coin as Geef counted them out, and stomped away. In just a short space of time, the two adversaries had created their own special routine. A social dance of sorts, like two grumpy bumblebees butting heads over a hollyhock.

Geifermann produced a small blue bottle, no larger than his thumb, from the pouch on his belt, and removed the stopper. "Poor old Rivvens, ye did 'ave a time of it... Oh well, this will fix him, right enough." The contents of the bottle fizzed slightly as he added it to Rivvens' drink. Sloshing it around to ensure it was thoroughly mixed in, he placed the tankard in front of Rivvens' stool and awaited his return.

He didn't have to wait long.

"Ugh," Rivvens shuddered as he returned to the table. "There are things in that outhouse ye wouldn't expect to see in a ghoul's bone pit. A fellow could catch somethin' nasty doin' his business in there."

"Thanks, fer the warnin'," Giefermann replied, rising from his stool. "It's my turn to visit the splash and dash."

"Have fun!" Rivvens chuckled. "Just remember, shakin' it more than twice is playin' with it!"

Geifermann rolled his eyes. "Oaf."

"Ahh," Rivvens sighed appreciatively upon spying his fresh flagon. "I do seem to be developing a taste fer this ale... down the hatch."

"Hold!"

Rivvens turned sharply in the direction of the barkeep, nearly spilling his drink down his front in the process. "What? He's paying!"

"Nay, lad," the innkeeper moved in so close that Rivvens could smell the rancid stew and hard spirits on the man's breath. "I saw yer *friend* slip somethin' in yer flagon. I don't like the looks of 'im, shifty eyes."

"Did he now?" Rivvens sighed, "The sly old bugger. Heh! Well, let's see how he likes his own medicine, shall we?" Taking a tankard in either hand, he switched the drinks then turned to the innkeeper and tapped his nose with his forefinger. "Not a word."

"Ha! me lips are sealed, don't ye worry. Serve 'im bloody right." Chortling to himself the innkeeper went back to his business, leaving Rivvens to take a gulp of ale and await Geifermann's return. Soon, the outhouse door slammed behind the drunken buffoon. Rivvens did his best to look oblivious to his friend's betrayal.

"Cripes, Rivvens, ye weren't kidding. There was a dead rat in one of the stalls.

"I know, I saw. The question is, did it crawl *into* the shitehouse or fall *out* of someone?"

Geifermann shivered. "Don't, ye'll sour me ale." Grasping the handle of his tankard... Geifermann took a gulp. "Ahh, like nectar."

Rivvens smirked. "Enjoyin' that?"

"Aye, 'tis a fine brew, indeed.

"Heh..."

Geifermann frowned. "What are ye giggling at?"

"Ah, nothing. Just a joke the innkeeper told me."

"What 'im?" Geifermann jerked a thumb in the innkeeper's direction. "Old chuckles over there? I wondered why he was grinning like an old skull. Damn, that's ghoulish... What was the joke?

"Oh, ye wouldn't get it, it was kind of... situational. Anyway, let me tell ye about the temple of Tsathoggua."

"Go on, then," Geifermann leaned forward expectantly. "Get on with it...."

* * *

Night had fallen once more by the time Rivvens reached the banks of the river Yann at the base of the Mloon Ranges. It had been two days since he had left the pedlar convoy on the Yann and Stoney Desert border. They had continued west into the desert itself where he had taken a route through the southern Yann wetlands to where the valley rose steeply into a formidable range of mountains. Peering up at the snow-capped peaks, he thanked Nodens that he didn't have to climb them. Pausing to refill the skein he kept for water from the fast-flowing river that shimmered like crystal under the twin suns that beat down from on high.

Before leaving the convoy, Rivvens had purchased a new knapsack and several ropes and climbing tools to replace those lost to the zoogs. He was just lucky that he kept his coin hidden in a compartment in the heel of his left boot. If he had lost that too, he'd have been forced to try and sell sexual favours... not that he would have got much of a price for those. All in all, he was on a run of luck that he put down to fussing over the fat tabby at *The Cotter's Lament.*

"Hear me, Puss, I'll buy ye a nice fat fishy next time I'm in town, ye have my word."

After splashing water on his face and finding a tree to hide under, he sat down and studied the map that the peddler-woman had drawn for him. So far, it had proven to be accurate, so he had no need to question it now. This left him with something of a choice. He could take a longer, more arduous path over the foothills and approach the hidden glade where the temple was situated from above. Or, he could take the more direct route along the river through the abandoned village of Poroth-Yip. It seemed an easy decision to make. Before heading off, he pondered the peddler-woman's parting words... "Beware the Formless Spawn."

After taking a draft of wine, Rivvens stood, gathered his things, and set off down the riverbank. His first problem was to find somewhere to cross the river. The waters were deep with strong undercurrents, so he was going to need a bridge of some sort. As luck would have it, a fallen tree stretched from one bank to the other began to become visible in the distance. He checked his map and peered through his spyglass, it appeared to be right outside the abandoned village. Once again thanking his lucky tabby for his good fortune, he pressed on.

To the surprise of the thief, the old oak tree crossing the mighty Yann River was secured in place with wooden pegs and had ropes on either side as makeshift rails. Not looking down at the speeding waters for fear of vertigo, Rivvens hopped onto the bridge gripping one of the ropes and shuffled crab-like to the other side. Despite the age of the fallen tree, it was sturdy and gave him no trouble. Soon, he was dusting his hands off on his cloak and peering down the weed-choked path leading to Poroth-Yip.

Not much was known about the village, at least by Rivvens, except that it had once been a thriving farming community and that its denizens simply vanished overnight. The *Ulthar Gazette* had reported that a traveller had come across the deserted village one morning to find places set for dinner complete with spoiled food. It looked like, whatever had prompted the exodus, the people of Poroth-Yip had left in one heck of a hurry. Even the village's livestock had disappeared. There wasn't a single sign of life.

Rivvens, erring on the side of caution, stuck to the skeletal shadows cast by the dead yew trees that lined the avenue. It was strange, it wasn't just the trees, everything approaching Poroth-Yip seemed to be dead. The weeds, crops, and grass, all were withered and yellow. It was as though the whole area had been stricken by some strange blight."

"I 'ope it's nothin' to do with the temple," Rivvens muttered through gritted teeth as he reached the first dwellings.

The architecture of Poroth-Yip was curious in and of itself. The habitats were unlike most Yannish structures, which tended towards decadent opulence, and were more akin to the basic desert-dwellings of Khem. Simple box-like houses with sagging gambrel roofs sat at odd angles to the road surrounded by a pasture that had long since gone to ruin. Rivvens peered through the window of an old farmhouse. It looked as though it hadn't been touched since the lady of the house had set the table. The oddest thing about it was that Rivvens, even on such a brief inspection, could see several items of monetary value... so, why the heck hadn't the place been looted for all its worth?

"Somethin' ain't right about this place..."

Almost as an answer, an odd scrabbling sound from a nearby barn chilled him to the marrow.

Rivvens bit his lip and stayed silent, waiting for another sign of life. He didn't have to wait long. The odd noise was followed by several more from the pasture behind him. Turning slowly, he peered into the dead grass just in time to see something disappear down a burrow. He would have loved to believe it was a simple gopher or rat but he would have been deluding himself. For a start, this wasn't small and furry... it was long and slimy. His Adam's apple bobbed as he swallowed hard. The land around him started to vibrate, almost imperceptibly, something vast was burrowing towards him. Rivvens cursed... he had figured out what had happened to the people of Poroth-Yip.

"Zoog's balls... dholes!" Knowing that there was no hope in standing and fighting, he turned tail and pelted towards the nearest verandah. He reached it just as one of the colossal pale worms broke the surface of the road, snapping its jagged-toothed maw in anticipation. Rivvens froze as it disappeared back under the soil. He padded slowly through the door of the house and mounted the stairs. Each one creaked and groaned as he made his way to the landing. Once on the upper floor, he stopped and took the first of several deep breaths. He was safe, for the time being.

There was one big problem facing him now. As it stood, he was trapped in a decaying farmhouse with dwindling supplies and a plethora of squirming horrors below his feet. Cursing his situation, he moved to the back window. "Oh, thank Nodens..."

Just over a small patch of scrubland, were the foothills of the Mloon Ranges. All he had to do was make it to the rocky plateau and he was safe. Even dholes, mighty as they were, couldn't penetrate solid granite. Cringing as the window creaked as he slid it open, Rivvens peered out and discovered a flat roof to his left covering the kitchen. Swinging his leg out of the window and swinging himself over, he crouched on the flat roof and stared at the dusty ground, searching for any sign of movement.

All was still. As tempting as it was to believe that the dholes had given up the hunt, he knew that wasn't the case. Dholes were notorious for their patience, even going as far as *starving out* their prey. Rivvens had heard horror stories about what even a single dhole could do to a town. Some years earlier, the Vale of Pnath had been plagued by the creatures. They had been thought to have been wiped out by sorcerers using Mnar stones. It appeared that some escaped.

"I can't stay here forever," Rivvens whispered to himself as a way to shake himself out of his reverie. "I need a distraction."

In yet another moment of serendipity, Rivvens happened to possess a small blasting charge. Geifermann had given him one, along with the special gloves, in case the entrance to the temple proved inaccessible. When he replaced his lost items at the caravan, he remembered the explosive at the last second and purchased a small globe of black powder and a box of *Cthugha's Fury* matches.

Striking the sulphurous head of a match against the sandpaper along the side of the box, Rivvens touched the flame to the fuse then lobbed the explosive as far as he could towards the first building. As soon as it hit the soil, the ground started to shake. Several furrows appeared from under the walls of the house and began to trace their way towards the noise. Rivvens crept to the end of the roof and lowered himself noiselessly to the floor.

Boom!

Rivvens started to sprint towards the rocks. The charge had done its job, but the distraction wouldn't last long. An ultrasonic wail echoed throughout the valley. Rivvens smiled, it looked like he had at least injured a couple of his hunters. This moment of joy was fleeting. In the next heartbeat, the furrows changed direction and began to trace lines in his direction. One dhole broke the ground, gliding through the air like a Cerenarian flying fish before plunging back underground.

With his heart fixing to explode, Rivvens flung himself the last couple of metres onto the plateau as one of the dholes made a snap for his right boot. He twisted through the air, landing hard on his back, driving the air from his lungs. The dhole wasn't going to give up its meal that easily, and started to slither onto the rocks. Rivvens scrambled back, coughing and spluttering. As the worm reared up and prepared to strike, he drew his sword and sliced it neatly in two.

Thanking Nodens that it had only been a juvenile - adults would have simply brushed off the attack without a scratch - the lucky thief dragged himself to his feet using a large boulder for support and limped further up the slope and out of danger. At the summit, he realised, to his immense joy, that he had accidentally found the entrance to the temple of Tsathoggua.

It was right where the old woman had said it would be, at the base of the mountains, nestled betwixt a shelf and a mass of fallen rocks. Rivvens nearly walked straight past it and would have done had he not spotted a roughly-hewn stone idol in the shape of a winged toad. Tearing aside the mass of tangled weeds and deadfall branches that choked the entrance, Rivvens prepared for the final part of his adventure. Constructing a torch from some of the debris at his feet and then lighting it, he cautiously went inside.

A foul stench like rotting meat nearly choked him as he

walked slowly down a narrow passage. Rivvens tore a strip of fabric from the bottom of his cloak and held it over his airways. The entrance had led to a sloping corridor, the walls of which ran with moisture. Thick fungal growths climbed towards the ceiling giving it a fleshy aspect. It was like being in the mouth of some awful beast. It continued for around half a mile under the mountain, getting hotter and hotter with each step.

The humidity was stifling and he began to feel somewhat like a steamed clam. Mercifully, he soon found himself in a large chamber with a flat black stone to the rear flanked by two looming statues of Tsathoggua. Aside from that, and a carpet of bones leading from the entrance to the altar, the room was bare. Rivvens thought his quest had been in vain until he spotted his prize sitting in the centre of the altar.

"At bloody last! I'm gonna want payin' double fer this, Geef."

It was just as Geifermann had described. On the altar sat a small silver casket that was fused to the stone. Rivvens tried to lever it off with his dagger to no avail. The damned thing simply wouldn't budge. In the end, he gave up and smashed it open with the hilt of his blade. A wide grin spread across his bewhiskered jowls. There it was, glistening in the flickering torchlight...

The Toad Stone.

* * *

"Show me!" Geifermann was so excited that he nearly knocked his tankard flying with his wild gesticulation.

"Not so fast, me old mucker," Rivvens replied in menacing tones. "I 'ave a bone to pick with ye first.

Me? Um... why?

Because, ye duplicitous sack of zoog droppings, Ye never told me about the spawn of the sleeping god."

"Eh?"

"Don't play dumb, Geifermann. I'm talking about the formless spawn of Tsathoggua!"

Geifermann's eyebrows knitted together like two caterpillars wrestling. "Look, Rivvens, I swear, I have no idea what ye are talkin' about!

Rivvens shook his fist in Geifermann's face. "What I'm talking about, is the big black ooze monster that came slurping and slithering out of the shadows! I screamed like a little girl and lobbed the torch at it. The damn thing just swallowed it up. So, there I was, running fer me life from a bloody great blob! It's a damn good job that fungus stuff on the walls was luminous or I'd never 'ave navigated the tunnel without coming a cropper."

Rivvens paused for a swig of ale then fixed Geifermann with an accusatory look. "I ran like a ghoul when the gravedigger's in town and managed to get me hairy arse out of there just in time, Luckily fer me, it turns out that those horrors don't like sunlight."

"Look," Geifermann held up his hands in surrender. "I swear, I didn't know about the big blob thing, Rivvens. My client never mentioned anything about *formless spawn*, or whatever you called it."

"Aye, well," Rivvens sniffed. "I'll choose to believe ye... this once."

"Thank you," Geifermann finished his drink, paused, then grinned like an excited child "Can I see the stone now?"

"Aye, Just a moment, it's in me new knapsack," he started to rummage in the depths of his bag, finally locating the stone and dropping it onto the table with a clatter. As he did this, he noticed Geifermann acting furtively. "Hey... what are ye up to over there?

"Putting on gloves."

Rivvens frowned. "Why?"

Because," Geifermann sighed and waggled his gloved fingers at his friend. "I told ye at the time that ye shouldn't touch it with ye bare skin. That's why I gave ye the special gloves."

"Aye, I know, but I lost the damn things, remember?" Rivvens suddenly looked alarmed. "Why? ... Why shouldn't ye touch it with bare skin?

"It's probably nothin' to worry about, but the *Book of Eibon* says that the stone can *change* the person into a *servitor* of the toad god."

"What?" Rivvens exploded. "Servitor? What the hell do ye mean, *servitor*? Surely, ye don't mean... formless spawn?"

"Um..." Geifermann tried his best to find an answer that wouldn't further enrage his companion. "Possibly... or, maybe a Voormis?"

"What?" Rivvens roared and nearly flipped the table as he shot out of his seat.

"Look, calm down, Rivvens, fer Nodens' sake. Don't get excited. It's probably a load of zoog droppings anyway. Did ye *feel* anything when ye touched it?"

Rivvens' brow furrowed as he tried to recall. "Um, not really. Well, a little tingle, perhaps..." He paused, then sighed, letting his head sag. "Okay, it burned me hand. What the hell is it doing to me, Geifermann? Tell me, or I'll slit yer throat right now!"

As Rivvens drew his blade, much to the surprise of the inn's patrons, Geifermann played his trump card. "Calm down. It will all be alright. I figured ye must have touched it when ye said about losing the gloves. I've taken care of it."

"What the hell do ye mean, *taken care of it?*"

Geifermann stood and clasped his friend by the shoulders in an attempt to sit him down. "Fer the love of Nodens, calm down. The ghoul said that adrenaline can speed up the *change*. That's why I didn't mention it before. I had to get the antidote into ye before ye started panickin'!

"Antidote? What blasted antidote?"

"Never fear, yer old pal, Geifermann, has yer back. I slipped it into yer drink when ye went fer a slash.

"What?"

"Yeah," Geifermann grinned. "You've been drinking the antidote this whole time."

Rivvens buried his head in his hands. "Oh, ye stupid bastard... no!"

"What's the problem, Rivvens, ye ungrateful bastard? I saved ye, why aren't ye happy?"

"Because... I switched the tankards when *ye* went fer a slash. I thought ye were tryin' to poison me."

Geifermann looked wounded by the accusation. What, me, poison ye? Never... Ye are like a brother to me."

"Didn't ye strangle yer brother?"

"Aye, well," Geifermann shrugged, "he was a thief and a scoundrel who got what was comin' to him. I'd never do that to ye! Never!"

"Ugh," Rivvens clutched his stomach and doubled over, his face growing clammy. "I don't feel..."

Geifermann started to panic. "It will be alright, my old friend, just ye wait an' see. Old Geifermann will save ye."

"How?"

Geifermann looked in his tankard, there were only the tiniest of dregs. "Um... Ah, I know, I'll find the ghoul and get another dose. Ye'll be right as rain in no time. Ye'll see...

Rivvens groaned in agony, clutching the table for support.

"Rivvens, are ye alright? Hang in there, me old mucker."

Rivvens let out a strangled wail and then dropped to the floor like a stone.

"Rivvens? Talk to me, Rivvens!"

As Geifermann dashed around the table, Rivvens sat up and let out a mind-blasting stream of guttural syllables. *"Arrrrrgggggggggggg... hup n'ghftog ebumna throdog Tsathoggua nafl'fhtagn!"*

Geifermann leapt back as his friend's skin turned black and oily, his clothes melting away in the blink of an eye. "Holy Nodens, save me!

The thing that had been Rivvens rose and swelled into a giant black ball of inky protoplasm.

"What the hell is that *thing?"* The Innkeeper cried as people started to scream and dash for the door. "Get it outta' me bloody inn, this instant!"

"Out!" Geifermann bellowed over the din. "Everybody, run!"

As the innkeeper drew a longsword from under the bar, the formless spawn lashed out with a whip-like pseudopod that coiled around his neck and tore his head from his body. The wound steamed as the spawn started to dissolve its first meal. Next, it turned its attention to Geifermann...

"No! Keep back. Ye wouldn't hurt yer old pal, Geifermann, right?... Rivvens? ... RIVVENS? ... ARGHHHH!

As screams and ghastly slurping noises sang out into the violet skies above Ulthar, the plump tabby cat finished wiping its whiskers before giving the inn a final look and stalking off into the shadows. It needn't have ended this way. If only The Lucky Thief had remembered to bring him that fishy he'd promised...

WIND

- Russell Smeaton

Einar wrapped his furs closer around him and huddled closer to the fire. Not for the first time he regretted taking this job. Even though born in the unforgiving mountains of the frozen North, he'd left many years ago. However, a few weeks back, whilst hunched over a mug of sour ale in a squalid tavern, he couldn't resist the offer of gold to escort two priests. They wanted to take pilgrimage to a temple to some god he'd never heard of, let alone pronounce. But he knew the mountain area and knew it was devoid of life, strong winds and harsh weather making sure of that. Legends of Frost Giants were just that - stories to keep children in bed at night. No one had seen so much as a footprint, let alone an actual giant. So, whilst it would be a miserably cold trip, the only danger might be the occasional desperate wolf or two.

Meagre belongings packed, the small party had quickly reached the forests of the foothills, towering snow-capped peaks looming in the distance. Einar felt no feelings of nostalgia to be back home. The place was cold, harsh and unforgiving. When he'd left, his father had grunted something about making sure he kept his feet dry and his sword clean before going back to hammering horseshoes. Besides, his companions kept up an endless stream of babbling conversation. He listened in, trying to work out what was so important. In his home village, people only had one god without a name, who never listened anyway. Everyone knew there was no point erecting even a simple stone shrine, let alone build a temple.

The priests had introduced themselves as Thron and Babel. Thron was clearly the leader, old and leathered from many years in the sun. In contrast, Babel could only have been fifteen summers or so, skin so unblemished it practically glowed. He hung off every word Thron spoke. As Einar listened, they were on their way to pay homage to a god called Ithaqua. The name rang a bell to Einar, but he didn't really care for the gods. Thron explained that by honouring Ithaqua, they could survive in any weather, including the bone-chilling cold they were currently experiencing. Clearly, neither Thron nor Babel were used to the cold, huddled together, shivering so hard in their furs their very bones clacked together.

Einar threw on another log onto the fire.

"Thank you kindly, Einar," said Thron, smiling a well-worn smile. Babel said nothing, dark eyes keeping a wary eye on Einar. "Do you know how much further? This cold is no friend to an old man,"

"Not much further now," grunted Einar. "We go over this hill, cross the lake and then climb Mount Ezra. There we'll find your temple." He didn't mention that if the lake wasn't frozen, they'd have to add an extra day or two. As they sat near the fire, the wind started to moan and sigh. It was going to be a colder than usual night if the wind picked up. Einar glanced up at the sky, already dark. Stars twinkled high above, indifferent to the frozen earth below. Oddly, the trees remained motionless despite the now howling wind. He frowned, looking around. Thron and Babel were so close to each other, they may have been embracing. Neither showed any effects of the wind. Babel's long lank locks remained flat to his scalp as did Thron's grey cloud-like hair. Einar shrugged. Maybe they had camped in some kind of lee, sheltering them from the wind. Putting it out of his mind, Einar wrapped himself up in his furs, and settled down to sleep.

He was awoken sometime later. Dawn was beginning to creep up, changing the sky from black to dark purple, but it was too early to be awake. Stars still flooded the night sky and the fire gently smouldered. Einar sprang to his feet, senses sharpened by many years of living by his wits. Something had woken him, and he stood motionless, peering around, trying to identify the culprit. Thron and Babel lay across the fire, snoring in their furs, oblivious to everything. The wind still howled, but that wasn't what had woken him. Prowling round the camp, he could see nothing untoward, and contemplated the possibility of catching some more sleep. Just then a noise like a thousand handclaps shattered the silence.

The source of his disturbance finally made itself clear. Birds. Thousands of birds. A clacking, squawking chaos of feathers, darkening the morning sky as they flew closer to the camp. Flying in the same direction, away from the mountains, Einar had to duck as the birds swooped past, barely missing him. Thron and Babel woke, eyes widening in confusion as the birds made their exodus.

"What's going on?" demanded Thron.

"Something has got them spooked," Einar replied. "Never seen anything like it."

Eventually the last of the birds passed, and the forest fell back into silence. Morning brightened the sky, and the three of them packed their belongings. The forest felt eerie and unearthly and not even the usually garrulous Thron spoke. Setting off, they trudged through the trees, the cold making bones ache and chests heave. As the forest thinned, the lake ahead glittered in the sunlight. Einar hoped and prayed to whatever gods he could remember that the lake be frozen. It was cold out here, colder than he remembered, and he wanted to make this trip as quick as possible.

Einar was in luck. A thick ice covered the lake, and he gingerly edged himself onto its surface to test its strength. The ice creaked and groaned, but held fast. He carefully walked on further and gave an experimental stamp of a fur clad boot. Satisfied, he motioned for the others to join him, and soon they were walking in single file across the frozen lake. A cold wind blew down from Mount Ezra, lifting a fine powdery snow off the ice. Thron and Babel took to clinging to each other to stop from slipping on the treacherous surface as Einar forged ahead, keeping an eye out for tell-tale cracks.

Except for a few bruised behinds, they reached the other side of the lake without incident. Setting up camp, the small party decided to bed down for the night. The days were short this close to winter, and the previous night's disturbance had put everyone on edge. Einar cut a hole in the ice and managed to catch a few fish for supper, which were soon cooking over the small fire. The forest remained cold and still, aside from the occasional creak of a frosty tree.

Conversation lulled as they sat around the campfire, staring into the flames, each in a world of their own. Einar didn't mind. He preferred the silence to the old man's incessant yabbering about Ithaqua and the powers that would soon be bestowed upon them. Night crept up and swallowed them in darkness. Throwing a few more logs onto the fire for the night, the trio wrapped themselves in their furs and settled down. Tomorrow they would push on, and begin the ascent of Mount Ezra to reach the temple of Ithaqua.

With the darkness came the wind again, howling in earnest. Einar lay listening to it gibber and moan. It was the same as the night before. Yet despite the noise, he could feel no breeze; the smoke from the fire drifted straight up into the night sky, stars glinting like diamonds. Not a cloud was in sight, and the trees remained motionless. Unable to sleep, he went to relieve himself behind a tree. Away from the fire, the forest loomed large and felt full of danger. Of a sudden, goosebumps raised over Einar's arms and necks, causing him to reach instinctively for his sword. Standing motionless, the warrior strained his eyes and ears to try and identify the source of his anxiety, yet the trees refused to give up their secrets and the only sound was the incessant wind.

As he turned his back on the forest to go back to the campfire, the ground shook, and Einar cursed as he fought to keep his balance. Straightening up, he raced back to the camp. Avalanches were never to be taken lightly, even this side of winter. The two pilgrims were wide awake, clutching each other and looking around with wide eyes. The ground shook again, though not so hard as before. If it was an avalanche, it wasn't near to them. Einar felt the knot in his stomach unclench somewhat. Stoking up the fire once more, the three of them sat around, unable to sleep, as the ground continued to shake, the sound slowly receding as morning crept up.

The next day, as they were packing, Einar took one last look at the lake. Huge snowy boulders had been discharged from the mountain, missing their campsite entirely. In lieu of any gods of his own, he thanked the stars for keeping them safe. Thron obviously thanked Ithaqua and a pantheon of other gods whose very names made Einar's skin crawl.

They took off into the forest and up the mountain, keen to reach the temple before nightfall. The going was steep, but the path clear. They encountered no other pilgrim on their way, but Einar couldn't shake the feeling they were being watched. The trees thinned the higher they walked up the slope, and so did the air. Clearly struggling, Thron stubbornly pushed on, his breathing sounding like a child's rattle. Einar couldn't help but admire him as he stumbled up the mountain, leaning heavily on Babel.

They all smelled it before they saw it. A sweet, coppery stench that lingered in the thin air. Babel took a deep breath with a quizzical expression, trying to work out what the odour was. Thron looked pensive and Einar felt himself reach for his sword once again. The sight came into view as they reached the top of a small rise - a steaming pile of animal remains, jumbled together in an untidy heap. Einar approached, keeping his eyes on the few surrounding trees. The meat was still fresh, whatever had happened, had happened recently. Blood seeped into the surrounding snow, thickening as the cold started to take hold. Einar peered into the mound, making out the furry carcasses of all manner of creatures - wolves, rabbits, even a bear. Whatever had done this was big, and strong. He thought again about those childhood legends of frost giants and felt the hairs lift up on the nape of his neck.

The group moved on quickly, not wishing to tarry any longer around the mound of death and destruction. The path led onwards up the mountain, and it wasn't long before they started to spot signs of what could only be symbols or totems for the temple. Einar didn't recognise the signs that were carved into trees. As he traced the sigils with a dirty fingernail, his skin itched and he soon stopped, wanting to get away from the place as fast as possible.

It wasn't long after that, that the sun slid down behind the mountains, and the first stars began to stud the night sky. With no temple in sight, it looked as though they were destined to spend yet another night out in the open. The idea was not attractive, given the memory of that bloody pile of still fresh, ravaged flesh, and so it was no small thing when they spied a glow in the trees a small distance ahead. Tired and cold as they were, they forced themselves on and, sure enough, there was what had to be their destination - the temple of Ithaqua.

Carved directly into the rock, it was not the fanciest of temples. After the opulent temples of the dark and steamy south, this was positively spartan. Even so, the thought of spending a night in the security of a sanctuary made it seem the most palacious destination Einar had ever seen. As they neared the temple entrance, robed priests came out to welcome them. With genuine smiles of greeting, the acolytes took the pilgrims' belongings and ushered them into the dark interior. Einar wasn't fooled... he'd spotted thick, corded muscles on the arms that peeked out from under the grey woollen robes. These holy men could surely look after themselves if need be.

The interior was as plain as the exterior. Clean, but bare of the usual entrapments of temples and holy places. Yak candles spluttered in small alcoves on the walls, creating a flickering light. As they walked deeper into the temple, Einar spotted the same cryptic symbol he'd seen earlier, this time carved into the stone. There was little noise in the chambers, none of the chants that normally went hand and foot with these types of places. The only sounds were the incessant babble as Thron waxed lyrical about Ithaqua and their echoing footsteps as they walked deeper into the temple.

Eventually even Thron stopped talking, and they continued in silence. That's when Einar started to hear it - the soft hum of the wind. At first, he could barely make it out, but once he noticed it, the sound increased in volume, getting louder with every step. He became aware that the path gently sloped upwards, finally opening out into a large, well-lit chamber. After the darkness of the bare corridors, it took Einar a moment to adjust to the light. When he did, the first thing he spotted was the large statue in the middle of the chamber. Vaguely human in shape, it towered above them. Made to resemble some kind of shaggy beast, straw had been used to mimic hair. As his eyes moved up the statute, they finally rested on the face. The eyes were made of the two biggest rubies Einar had ever seen. They sparkled warmly in the light of the chamber.

A large priest awaited, Einar guessing that this was the leader of the sect. Thron and the priest were soon deep in hushed conversation. With nothing else to do, the guide contented himself with idle fantasies of what he would do if he stole the rubies. They would fetch a pretty penny, and he might even be able to buy a bit of land somewhere. A cough behind him made him start, and he saw the acolytes looking at him, smiling, but with steel eyes. One look at those muscled arms put all such daydreams out of Einar's mind. He straightened up and waited for Thron to finish conversing with the head priest.

After what seemed like an eternity, Einar was led to a small chamber that would be his bed for the night. Whilst not the most comfortable, he'd slept in far worse, and the soup and bread was fresh and delicious. Stomach full, he laid himself down on the firm pallet of straw and felt himself doze off.

He awoke in the dark. The howl of the wind had picked up whilst he had been sleeping, even this deep inside the temple. Senses alert, he sat up and dressed with quick, efficient movements. He stole out of his chamber, crouched like a tiger ready to spring into action. Quickly finding his way into the central chamber, Einar was surprised to see Babel hanging off the face of the statue, prising out the rubies with a dagger. He'd already removed one and was working on the second. Thron was below, encouraging him to work faster.

Einar realised he had been duped. These weren't pilgrims, in search of the fabled Ithaqua, they were common temple robbers, no better than himself! The wind by now had worked itself up to a fever pitch, screaming like a banshee. Over its howl, he heard the pounding footsteps as the priests came running. Thron yelled at Babel, who promptly fell from the statue, hitting the floor with a sickening crack. Einar grimaced as Babel's leg twisted at an unnatural angle, the boy yelling out in agony. Thron bent forward, at first, Einar thought, to help Babel. Still, he wasn't surprised to see Thron grab the stolen ruby and run off down one of the corridors, leaving Babel to writhe on the floor, yelling for his companion to come back. His wide eyes fell on the warrior and he began imploring Einar to help instead. But before Einar could act, strong hands gripped his arms, and the world went black as something smashed into the back of his head.

Coming round, Einar found himself bound and trussed to a wooden stake. It was cold and bright. Looking round as best he could, he saw he was back at the frozen lake. Head buzzing and muscles aching, he tried to assess the situation. To his right, Babel was similarly strung up, but the boy was still unconscious, head hanging limply on his chest. The lad's leg stuck out at an awkward angle, clearly broken. On his left, Thron had also been captured and trussed up, but was awake, thrashing in a vain attempt free himself from his bonds.

All around the frozen lake the priests stood, silent and grim. They had disrobed and, despite the cold, stood naked. They parted ranks and the tall, thin head priest strode through the gap. Also naked, his body was painted with the sigil Einar had seen earlier. A murmur and swell of noise ran through the crowded acolytes, sounding much like the wind. The head priest made a gesture and the crowd fell silent. But there was that noise again - the howling of the wind, despite the still air. It increased in volume, becoming so loud Einar's ears felt close to bursting.

Just as he thought his ears were going to explode, he heard a cracking noise, like thunder, and he wondered if an avalanche was going to either save him or send them all to oblivion. It was neither. One of the boulders Einar had seen before slowly stood up, revealing a monster not dissimilar to the statue in the temple. As it uncurled, it seemed impossibly big, taller than the tallest priest, and soon towered above even the trees. The thing was covered in thick, mattered fur and Einar could smell the raw animal stench it gave off. Its facial features were all but hidden in the same shaggy fur, revealing little more than two huge red eyes that burnt like fire as it glared at the crowd. The creature tilted back its head, opening a huge, cavernous mouth. As Einar watched, the monster howled, revealing once and for all where the sound of the wind came from. Louder than ever, the ferocious howling noise seemed to go on and on, until all Einar wanted to do was crawl away and hide.

The howling suddenly stopped, and the crowd began chanting the name "Ithaqua" over and over, swaying and swooning in their adoration. Some began beating their chests, others fell to their knees, bowing in reverence. Thron, who had fallen silent at the sight of the beast, began his thrashings anew, desperate to escape. The beast turned and faced him. With one shaggy hand that was all too humanoid, it reached out and plucked Thron, stake and all, from the ground. Thron seemed tiny in that huge hand as he wriggled and squirmed. The thing brought Thron up to eye level and stared at him, turning him this way and that. Einar gave himself a moment of hope, wondered if the being was simply curious as to what this bug was in front of him. But moments later, the creature bit down on Thron, severing him in two. Blood and entrails spilled everywhere, soaking the priests below, sending them into even more of a frenzy. Throwing away the remains of Thron, like a child throwing away a broken toy, the beast started scooping up priests, stuffing them into its mouth, biting and chewing without discernment.

Chaos erupted. This was clearly not what the priests were expecting, and they started to flee in blind panic. Some ran into each other, skidding on the now bloody surface of the lake. Others simply stood, staring blankly up as mind and bladder dribbled away. The demon was everywhere, misshapen hands red with gore, as it continued to devour the crowd. Torsos, arms and legs soon littered the scene and Einar turned his head as best he could to avoid seeing more. Eventually, the beast slowed, rubbing its stomach, seemingly satisfied with its gluttonous feast. Einar and Babel had been forgotten, still tied up on their stakes. Einar felt his mind twist and squirm as he took in the bloody aftermath. Worse than any battle he had seen, the lake was a mess of broken bodies. Amongst the human wreckage few priests still lived, moaning for help. The beast casually sauntered over to them, still rubbings its gut, and with one fluid movement stomped down hard, crunching their bones beneath its broad foot.

Having remained unconscious throughout the entire massacre, Babel took this moment to wake up, moaning as he came to. Einar tried to shush him. He prayed to whatever gods he could think of to let the beast be full and sleepy. Alas it seemed the gods had abandoned him, and the beast turned its great shaggy head towards the two of them. The beast approached, slowly, deliberately. Babel started screaming before his mind gave way, and he fell back into unconsciousness, head flopping against his chest. The monster flicked Babel's head with a thick hairy finger, like a cat playing with a ball, watching it roll one way then the next. It quickly bored of this game, effortlessly plucking the head off and throwing it over the trees, as steaming blood sprayed out of the ragged neck stump.

Then it turned its attention to Einar. The warrior held his breath. The stench that came off the demon was raw, thick and ripe. It also gave off heat, pulsating in waves so extreme they scorched Einar's face. The demon stood examining the human, shimmering in waves of heat. Einar felt the stake he was tied to shift ever so slightly. He tried twisting around a little, and was rewarded by the stake moving more noticeably. The demon looked down at its feet, which had sunk into the melting ice a fraction. Looking back at Einar, it bellowed at him, a carrion smell fit for hell and a noise like a gale to end all gales.

The scream proved to be Einar's saviour. The sheer force of it pushed him back far enough for the stake to become free of the ice. He didn't think twice and began running awkwardly for the tree line. The hot breath of the beast chased him, but he didn't look back. Against all odds, he reached the trees in safety. Just ahead, two blood splattered priests cowered in the snow, huddled together, either to try and keep warm or to keep from going insane. Making a beeline for them, he took in their wide-eyed stares and hoped they weren't too far gone. Luckily, they still had some wits about them and with trembling fingers helped free Einar of the stake. The three of them crouched for cover and peered through the trees at the now empty lake.

The monster was no longer visible. All that was left was the steaming mass of body parts. As Einar scanned the area for any danger, a crow flew down and started to peck at a ragged chunk of meat. Another crow swooped down, followed by another and soon the lake was alive with the welcome signs of bird life. Taking the return of the birds as a sign the demon had truly gone, Einar ventured out of the trees. The two priests scuttled around the edge of the lake, gathering discarded robes before disappearing into the forest.

As for Einar, he lingered for a while longer. He kicked through the robes to see if there was anything that might help him get back to civilisation, some food or even a coin or two. In doing so, he stumbled across Thron's satchel. He peered inside, heart picking up a notch. Sure enough, there was the stolen ruby, glinting in the cold sun. Pocketing it, Einar sauntered through the trees ,whistling all the while. Only when the wind sighed through the trees did he pick up his pace, vowing never to return to the frozen north ever again.

WIND

THE HAUNTER OF THE CATACOMBS

- Gavin Chappell

1.   The Death of Beauty

Talon was a thief.

This wasn't the way he"d envisaged his life, it was just something he was doing until something better came along. So, he was a thief. Oh, and sometimes he cut throats. Purses, too, on the more profitable nights. Or maybe none of that was true. Because Talon was also a liar. A thief and a liar. And a cutthroat. But this was only temporary. One of these days he would really be somebody.

Talon the Cutthroat, some people called him. But seldom twice. And even Talon the Rogue. He didn't like that either.

That night, that fateful night when it all went wrong, he was making his way through the Forest of Light in the direction of the holy Lawberg, not as a plaintiff, or a jury man, or even a sightseer, but as a thief. He had a plan to rob the ancient catacombs beneath the citadel, home to the mortal remains of

Lord Zennor's august predecessors. If he pulled off this job, it ought to net him enough coin to settle down, go straight, become a force to be reckoned with in some real line of work. That was what he thought. That was what he hoped.

No thief wants to be famous, it's bad for business, but how it had warmed his cockles to learn that he was notorious in some quarters. Thieves quarters, of course. In the stews and the brothels of the cities of the western continent, he was known to all the wrong people. Sometimes that was a help. Often it was more a hindrance.

Regardless, he had little to fear on that score, not in these parts. The wrong people simply didn't go near the Lawberg... except as prisoners.

Six times had the greater moon chased the lesser from the night sky before he finalised his plans. He much preferred the planning stage to the venture itself. Usually, the latter was either tedious - that was when the plan went off without a hitch - or terrifying and needlessly adventurous, leaving him reflecting, sometimes from the dank confines of a dungeon, that he was really getting too old for this. When the plan just didn't come together. When it all went wrong.

It was all going to go wrong tonight, far worse than it ever had before. But right at that moment, as he flitted from glowing tree to glowing tree, his eyes fixed on the Citadel of Justice that topped the Lawberg like an accusing finger pointed at a recalcitrant sky, he had no notion of quite how sour the plan was going to turn...

He pulled up sharply, hearing the clank of metal shod feet on rock. Darting into the cover of a glowing tree, careful to avoid contact with the radiant foliage, he peered out.

Coming up the path, the crash of their armoured feet providing a discordant counterpoint to the ceaseless tintinnabulation of the iridescent crystalline leaves, were two guards, bearing halberds. A patrol! Nothing he had gleaned from a dozen quiet enquiries had prepared him for this, patrolling guards in the Forest of Light. Its lethal vegetation was seldom traversed by any but the most rash. Gamblers. Daredevils. Those who would face all risks in return for a quick profit.

Yet here they were, and from the scales of justice emblazoned on their armour, he knew them for imperial guards of the High Council of the Lawberg, possibly even Lord Zennor's personal troop.

He sat tight in his hiding place and waited for them to pass. But what was this? Both had halted mid-path and were staring at the starry sky. Talon glanced upwards and that was when he spied what had alerted them.

Tumbling through the night towards the Citadel, clearly in trouble, was a tiny dot that abruptly resolved itself into that rarest of flying beasts, a hippogriff. On the back of the hippogriff sat an armoured figure.

Elenara Moonstar held on tightly to the reins of her steed as its wings beat the air. It spiraled wildly towards the landing platform on the citadel like a leaf in a storm. The hippogriff, perhaps the last of his kind, was severely wounded, the broken off shaft of an arrow jutting from his breast feathers.

Elenara's armour also showed signs of recent fighting, scored and battered as it was and even burnt in places. Her eyes were wide with horror as she struggled to guide her steed down. It was imperative she bring her message to Lord Zennor and the High Council. A terrible tale it would make.

At last, the hippogriff landed on the smoothly polished stone of the landing platform, a wide expanse big enough to hold hundreds of such mounts, hoofs clicking and clopping before he collapsed, sending Elenara sprawling undignifiedly on the stone. But as attendants hurried out from the citadel to aid her and her steed, she spared no thought for her own pride.

The hippogriff was dying.

Elenara had raised him from the egg. All the imperial paladins had reared their own hippogriffs-an inseparable bond was thus created, one that lasted until either paladin or hippogriff died. And even as an attendant helped her rise, and the rest tended to the mortally wounded beast, she knew they had reached that point. Bleakly, she accepted wine from the attendant, but it did little to wash away the pain.

One of the others approached her tentatively. "Ma"am," he said, his insect like mandibles clicking as he helped her remove her armour, "we"re very sorry. We were too late."

"He bore me long and far, through the dimensional gates," Elenara said with a sigh. "And already his wounds were mortal. I will see he is interred in the most ancient of the catacombs beneath the citadel. But just now I have urgent news. Where will I find Lord Zennor?"

"He and the High Council are gathered in the Chamber of Justice," clacked the attendant. "They await news of the war." His compound eyes were hard to read, but Elenara knew that he was curious himself. However, she refused to slake that unspoken curiosity. She could not tell him that Evil had utterly triumphed.

"I must go to them," she said. "But I will return to see that all is done as it should be for my steed." Fair locks whirling around her head like a lion's mane, she turned and strode across the platform towards the high ivory gates of the citadel.

The two guards were talking in an undertone. Talon was growing impatient. They stood between him and his destination, showing no sign of moving on. The hippogriff who had caught their attention was out of sight, no doubt having landed on the citadel above, although at this point it was impossible to see due to perspective.

With one hand Talon hunted about in the dry soil. Then his fingers closed what he had been searching for-a stone pebble. He flung it into the trees on the far side of the path. The clatter rang out harshly over the jingling of the leaves. Both guards whirled round.

"What in Ti's name was that?" one asked. Both had their backs to Talon now, but still their armoured forms blocked his path.

The other guard issued a challenge, but there was no response.

"We must investigate it," urged the first guard.

"No sense in us both going," said the other. "You go, but be cautious. I'll keep the path guarded. Remember, raiders have been sighted."

Talon tried not to giggle. One guard was now forcing his way through the glowing trees, halberd at the ready, searching for any sign of interlopers. But his companion remained, guarding the path. Talon considered trying to make his way through the trees, but he was unarmoured, and the crystalline leaves were sharper than any thorns. They would cut him to pieces before he had got a man's length further.

Only one thing for it. Silently drawing his long knife, he slipped out of his hiding place and padded across the rocks towards the guard. Still the man kept his back to him. This would be only too easy.

The guard stamped his feet. It was a cold night, and the steam of his breath issued from the ventail of his horned helmet. He gripped his halberd in one gauntleted hand and watched where his mate had gone. In the eerie light of the lesser moon, he could see little but the gleam of the man's armour.

Then something was on his back like one of the legendary vermin of the catacombs. Talon gripped the armoured man by the throat with his left forearm, forcing the ventail upwards. Instinctively the man caught Talon's arm in his gauntlets, metal fingers bruising his flesh. Cursing inwardly, Talon thrust his blade through the resultant gap, felt it slide slickly into flesh, gritted his teeth again as he jerked the knife across in a horizontal slash. As blood jetted from the guard's helmet a gargling cry of alarm burst from his lips, then he fell with a clatter.

His corpse lay in a heap of ironmongery, blood seeping sanguinely across the stones in the light of the lesser moon. The thief cursed. This was what he always hated. The plan had gone awry. That appalling, inhuman noise would have alerted the other guard, who even now could be heard blundering back through the crystalline vegetation. Not stopping to wipe his blade, Talon ran down the path in the direction of the catacombs entrance.

2.   The Solace of Shadows

Elenara strode into the council chamber, head held high, though her heart was heavy. She endured the questioning stares of the High Councillors as they gazed down at her from the serried ranks of seats, dwarfed as she was by the immensity of the chamber. A hush descended upon the robed figures.

She reached the bottom of the three steps leading to the podium. Lord Zennor sat upon his modest stone seat, watching her approach. She knelt on one knee, inclined her head.

"In the name of the Sword and the Ring, may I speak with his lordship?" she asked, her voice clear and carrying.

"Of course, child," said Lord Zennor. Was that anxiety lurking at the corners of his ice blue eyes?

Elenara ascended the steps, made another obeisance.

"Enough of this bowing and scraping, child," Lord Zennor said gruffly. "Please make your report in the usual fashion. Tell the High Council why it is that only you return from the thousand strong force that issued forth."

Tears threatened to manifest in her eyes. She turned to regard the whole chamber. A galaxy of eyes gazed back at her.

"My lord, august councillors, we paladins encountered the Sons of Darkness mere worlds away. Their army was vast, comprising of ranks upon ranks of hideous creatures, norns, and corrigans, dark knights and things for which there can be no name, only that they are horrors. We were desperate, seeing the smoking ruin they had made of that world, a once pleasant forested place known as Ebonvale. Grizzled General Melanicus led us in the fray, his armour glittering in the harsh sunlight of that dimension, his red cloak fluttering behind him like a banner. I did not see what happened to him, being beset myself by many foes. But when I saw how many had been lost I realised at last that we had no hope."

"Paladins were slain on that field?" asked a High Councillor.

"Paladins were lost," Elenara corrected him. "Some were slain, aye. But more were... altered. I saw the change come over them with my own eyes. Their gleaming armour grew black as if darkly corroded. Their eyes changed, their faces too. The hippogriffs also altered under the baleful influence of the black sun that rose above the field, became twisted and horrific, until they were the foulest of manticores and hippogriffs no longer.

"I saw in the end that it was hopeless, futile. A message must be sent to the High Council. I sought for someone who could go but could find no one. So I went myself. As I did, an arrow caught my hippogriff in the breast. He flew long and hard before he came to this dimension, this world... The exertion was too much for him. He died on my return."

"You fled the field?" another High Councillor taunted her. "Confess the truth! It was you who deserted your comrades!"

Elenara shook her head. "That is not true. Besides, by the time I commanded my hippogriff to fly for the dimensional gate, I had no comrades to desert. Do you not understand? It was the corrupting power of Evil... some spell, perhaps, some baleful influence of the black sun that shone above the field of fight. I remember the same story from when I was young, before I joined the paladins. Time and again have they set out against the Sons of Darkness. Time and again have few returned. All told the same tale.

"And now none but me, most recently raised to their ranks, is left. The corrupting rays of the black sun... the dark flame...

it is not just that paladins have been slain, they have been... converted. Gone to swell the ranks of evil. August councillors, my lord Zennor. Darkness devours light, night swallows the day. evil eats up good. Evil cannot be fought, for those who fight it can only do so by committing evil acts themselves. By fighting Evil, we join its ranks..."

Lord Zennor tugged furiously at his long white beard. "If what you say is true, child," he interrupted, "we have no defence against the Dark Ones. Our every endeavour will be futile. Evil must be fought, or it will consume us, and all the worlds. But only evil can fight evil. Were we to raise a new army, it would be in vain. The champions of Good cannot prevail, cannot hope to prevail."

"Only evil can fight evil..." Elenara repeated his words, gazing at him wildly. "Therein lies our hope! We must pit the forces of Evil against Evil itself."

"And how can we do that, child?" Lord Zennor chided. "How can we hope to induce Evil to fight against itself?" He rose stiffly to his feet, with the aid of his ornately carved staff. "This meeting is ended. We have heard enough. Return to your duties."

As the councillors rose, Elenara turned to depart.

"Where will you go now, child?" asked Lord Zennor gently.

"First I must see to the entombment of my hippogriff," she told him.

"Very well," said Lord Zennor. "When it is done, come to me in my chambers. There is something I would speak with you about..."

The clatter of armoured feet echoed from the singing trees as

Talon ran towards the catacombs. The guard was after him! He had been seen! Seldom had a job turned this sour before.

Down a narrow cutting in the stone he went, with the great cliff of the Lawberg rearing high overhead. The stone was wet and slippery, and the steps that had been cut into it in places were hard to traverse. But soon he was at the gates, which were of beaten brass, richly ornamented, and as tall as three men.

He paused, reaching into his shirt for the forged key. The tale of its procuring would be a long one, best saved for the tavern. He inserted it into the keyhole, then paused, about to turn it. The clatter of the guard's armoured boots was growing louder.

Talon looked over his shoulder, to see an armoured shape silhouetted at the far end of the cutting. At that moment the greater moon rose above the horizon, and the cutting was flooded with its yellow light.

Cursing, Talon turned the key and shoved at the gates. With a grinding and rumbling they slowly opened.

"Hold!" The voice was loud and booming, magnified in some way by the armour the guard wore. "Hold still and submit yourself to judgement!"

"Not likely, friend," said Talon. He could see only one hope for it. As the rocks rang to the sound of the guard descending, he gave the gates another push and shove. The one on the left slowly opened to a crack, and darkness seemed to ooze from the catacombs within.

Talon darted inside, seeing only darkness, feeling the cold of the tomb, smelling the spicy scent of flesh embalmed with natron. Into the darkness he hurtled, seeking only to lose his pursuer in the catacombs. Later he might be able to rob at will, but the richest and oldest tombs were on the lower level, and he would find them when he had the time and the leisure.

As he fled down the long, night black passage, he thought he heard strange scuttling noises from the rock above. Things were rumoured to lair down here in the darkness, despite the best attempts of the guards to cull them. Quite what things they were nobody seemed to know. Nobody who had met them had lived to tell the tale.

There was a great roaring crash from behind him. Talon spun round to see the gates had been forced fully open. A man stood in the arch, armoured arms akimbo, the light of the greater moon gleaming from his horned helmet and his halberd.

"Give yourself up and you will be treated according to your deserts," boomed the guard's voice. Hardly a persuasive argument, Talon thought wryly, as the moonlight flooded the high vaulted passage. Seeing in its gleam a doorway hewn from the living rock on the left-hand wall he darted inside, seeking the solace of shadows.

Colliding with a carved stone slab in the darkness, he halted. Glancing back at the doorway, he saw the light was increasing. But mingled with the cold glow of the greater moon was the flickering light of flame. He smelt smoke drifting down the passage. The guard had lit a torch, and was coming after him.

A tortured scream rang out, the torchlight winked out, and then there was only silence. For a long time Talon crouched beside the slab, eyes on the doorway, trying to control his shaking limbs.

What in the name of Zorn had happened to the guard?

3. Into the Labyrinth

Eventually, after an aeon when he had heard nothing but the distant drip of water, Talon crept out of the room of the carven slab and paused in the passage. All was silent and dark, except for the hazy moonlight but it did not reach as far as his position. A star winked in the darkness nearby. A fallen star? He caught a whiff of smoke.

Kneeling down, he discovered that what he had seen was the guard's torch, guttered down to an ember. He snatched it up and blew on it until this ember blossomed with new flames that illuminated the great vaulted passage. Above his head the shadows still swallowed up the light.

He held the torch high but saw nothing. No one. No sign of the guard, not so much as a bent vantbrace. He held the torch as high as he could, and still the light did not shine on an armoured form, alive or dead. But it stirred up movement somewhere in the shadows high above. Something scuttled across the unseen roof.

He turned and hurried deeper into the labyrinth.

He had tombs to loot this night. Riches to reap.

Elenara stood gazing down at the great carcase. Guards and attendants stood respectfully back as she crouched, stirred her hippogriff's dorsal feathers for one last time. The bird like head, once warm with life was cold, the body limp, no more than dead meat.

She rose, and made a curt gesture to the attendants. They moved forward jerkily, and lifted up the creature's carcase on a palanqueen of spears. One of the guards began to beat solemnly on a kettle drum. Elenara standing tall amongst them, they began to march down the flight of steps that led to the foot of the Lawberg, to the vaults where the hippogriff would be interred.

"And so passes the hope of the Citadel," she murmured to herself as she trod the stone steps solemnly, and the pounding of the drum sounded like the slow footsteps of a sombre giant. The hippogriff had been the last of his kind, just as Elenara was the last paladin fighting for the forces of Good. Rumour had it that a clutch of eggs was concealed in some part of the kingdom, but none knew where.

Once there had been a great, merry band of paladins, sworn to defend the worlds of Light from the encroaching Sons of Darkness. Now the rule of Good obtained in only one world, this world where the Lawberg stood in the light of the greater moon like a statue to some embodiment of justice. The drum sounded the death knell not only of her dearly loved mount but of the hopes of fairness and honesty and justice in all the dimensions, all the worlds.

She knew that Evil existed everywhere, and was to be found even on her own world, but in former days it had been countered by equal amounts of goodness. Now Good was beleaguered, forced back to this one world. And Evil had become so strong that it could not be fought. It was the age old moral quandary made manifest. How to take up arms against Evil without becoming that which one fights. From what she had seen in the battle, it was no longer a mere philosophical abstraction. Those paladins who had not been slain, their hippogriffs with them, had renounced their vows, joined the forces of Evil.

They reached the foot of the Lawberg where the Forest of Light cast its hazy glow in the moonlight, only to find that Evil had struck once more.

Talon had reached a crossroads. Holding his torch up high, he gauged his chances down each one of the dark passages. Each wall was lined with doors, which led into tombs like the one within which he had concealed himself. He had inspected each one to learn to his dismay that these must have been the resting places of paupers, or those so vowed to a life of poverty that their grave goods were non-existent.

Another likelihood was that these tombs had been rifled by long dead thieves. Some still had doors, but usually their hinges were corroded, even if they had not been forced by earlier rogues. It had been an easy matter to gain entrance, but the effort had not been worthwhile.

Something scuttled across the roof high above him.

Talon increased his pace. These catacombs had become home to creatures of dire provenance, lairing within the ice cold passages during the night. Nothing had shown so much as a mandible as yet, but he was beginning to speculate about the fate of the guard who had come after him. The guards and the paladins and other high up folk from the Citadel of Justice neglected these vaults. Or perhaps they allowed dangerous creatures to take up residence to deter thieves.

But Talon was no ordinary thief. No ordinary thief, and this was no ordinary theft. This was the one that would make him rich, rich enough to quit this life of stealth and sleight, set up in a respected profession that had convenient working hours. He rather fancied training to become a lawyer. But no, he wanted to give up being a thief, and what were men of law but the biggest thieves imaginable?

What else, then? A royal minister, that would suit him down to the ground. He would implement the policies of some great king, working for the greater good, taxing the populace to pay for his king's righteous wars, along the way taking the opportunity to put by certain funds that would never be missed... but no! He wanted to give up being a thief.

Then maybe, with all the gold and treasure he would amass tonight, he could buy himself a position as an archpriest. Lead the commonalty in prayers and sacrifices to Zorn or some other equally pompous deity. Tithe his flock to pay for his own luxurious life like all the archpriests did. But he wanted to give up being a thief.

Was there any line of work that was anything other than thievery writ large? He was in the wrong profession. And he wanted out.

Turning a corner, he saw that the passageway beyond widened into a long, broad hall. Carven niches lined the walls and in each niche was a statue, or the remains of one. Solemn, lordly faces gazed blankly down at the small thief as he crept beneath them, torch held high. Between each two sets of statues was a large stone doorway. And all but one was shut fast.

No detritus lay on the floor, no signs of neglect were visible on the walls, other than the inevitable stains of moisture. He had at last reached the deeper catacombs, the ones he had heard whispered about. Where the treasures lay stacked in great pyramids of gold, heaps of silver, mountains of rubies and emeralds and sapphires. With his left hand, he wiped his mouth dry from the drool that had unconsciously gathered there, as he approached the largest of the doors.

He searched for some kind of keyhole. At last he detected one high up, out of reach. Producing a slender rope made from dead women's hair he fitted it to a grapnel, then swung it round several times and cast it high so it wound itself round the statue to the left. Now he began to foot it up the doorway, holding the torch in one hand, until he was level with the keyhole.

The statue's hand looked as if it was intended to grip something, as if it had originally been depicted holding what, a spear? A flagpole? Grinning cheekily, Talon inserted his torch into its grasp.

These vaults were ancient, sturdily built, but the art of lock making had come on since those antique days. He examined the lock, probed it with lockpicks. It would take time, and it would hardly be comfortable, picking the lock one handed while hanging from a rope, but it would all be worth it. No thief had rifled these vaults in the thousand years since their construction.

He had just picked the lock and was gazing at the riches that surrounded the interred corpse within when a cry of horror echoed down the endless corridors and passages of the catacombs. It seemed as if it came from the direction of the main entrance, although sound travelled strangely underground. Talon panicked. Had someone found the gates open, or the dead guard he had left in the Forest of Light?

Perhaps it was that echoing cry that inspired the scuttling thing that had been trailing Talon to make its attack. After gathering its many legs to itself up where it hung from on the shadow cloaked ceiling, it sprang at him.

4. The Haunter of the Catacombs

The first Talon knew of the attack was when a heavy, chitinous weight struck him between the shoulder blades and he was knocked from his perch on the rope, falling helplessly to the hard stone floor. The thing attacked him in a frenzy, and he tried to fend it off despite the ringing in his skull.

Rolling on his back he looked upwards to snatch a glimpse of an immense creature with far too many long, hairy legs, a constellation of staring eyes, a pair of clacking mandibles oozing venom. All this in the flickering, uncertain light of the torch that remained held in the stone hand of the statue.

He managed to free his long knife and jabbed upwards, catching a lashing leg clumsily. Then he hacked back and forth, flailing in horror at the barely illuminated monstrosity. It snapped at him with its fangs, and he scrambled backwards with the aid of one hand while flailing at the creature with the blade in the other. His retreat was curtailed when his back collided with the stone door of the vault.

"So you're the haunter of the catacombs," he said, gazing back into those staring idiot eyes clustered above the mouthparts. It must have been this creature that had attacked the second guard, carrying him off to its cobwebbed lair high overhead.

It struck again. Talon lurched to one side to avoid its fangs but it caught him a glancing blow to the shoulder. He felt no pain, only a light punch such as a hearty man might give in fun. But when he stabbed at the many eyes, a wave of nausea overcame him and he fell to one knee. The knife slipped from his hand, skipping and clattering across the stone floor, vanishing out of the ring of light afforded by the torch.

His opponent, fat and hairy, chitinous and glistening, lowered itself onto him, crushing him down to the floor. This job was really going wrong, he reflected as he lay helpless and paralysed. It should have been easy. He had planned well, done his research...

As the thing industriously wrapped him in bone white, sticky silk that oozed from the rear of its abdomen, he cursed the paladins. What did they think they were doing, allowing wild and dangerous animals to lair in these vaults? It was downright negligent of them. What would their ancestors think...?

Numbness crept through his brain. Everything seemed to happen so slowly. Aeons passed, and still he was being enfolded in silk, until he resembled some antiquated mummified king of the kind he had seen in the vault. He could no longer move his eyes, although he could see perfectly well until a greyness began to swim up on the sides of his vision.

Almost the last thing he was aware of was a clatter of metal shod feet which he felt through the stone floor rather than heard. Then the impression of a kind of lightning strike. The creature jerked as if it were a puppet and the puppet master was going into spasm. Absently, Talon noticed some kind of war hammer jutting from its head. Darkness swamped his mind.

"Then this is he, child."

Talon didn't understand. Oh, the words made sense, spoken in a rich, rolling, sonorous voice, a little crackly with old age. But what in the name of Zorn did the speaker mean? The sentence was so vague as to be meaningless. He tried to say so, but somehow he couldn't open his mouth. He tried to struggle, but he couldn't move. He felt nothing, saw nothing.

It was as if he were nothing but a disembodied consciousness, hanging in the dark void. Talon had never believed in ghosts and spirits, but was that what he had become? Was he now an ethereal spirit? He ought to panic at the notion but he felt nothing. No emotion. He was numb in every sense.

And yet he could hear.

"Yes, my lord. He who killed one guard and led another into the grasp of the arachnid."

The new voice was female, strong, vibrant, spirited, assertive. Humourless. He didn't think there was much hope of him sharing a flask of wine with its owner, followed by some intimate conversation in the private booth of a tavern.

"Now the attendants have finished stripping him of the spider silk, we will be able to bring him round for questioning. Happily you stumbled on him in the catacombs just before the arachnid began to suck out his juices. Now he can face justice."

"Yes, Lord Zennor. Had I not slain the beast, he would be a withered husk like the guard we found. Those catacombs would be purged of such horrors, had we the means."

Lord Zennor! Talon was in the presence of one of the most powerful men in the empire, the Lord of Lawberg, Chief Judge of the Citadel of Justice. He avoided judges at the best of times, and this was distinctly not the best of times. As for the other voice. Was this female the one he had to thank for his life?

"It has been tried. But perhaps it is better we do not slay them," Lord Zennor said, his voice coming closer. "They do not trouble us in the citadel, and they are effective guards against those who would come to the catacombs to rob and plunder."

Talon felt a flash of pain. It came from where his shoulder ought to be. Gradually, feeling returned. His hearing improved, the greyness that had obscured his vision shrank back like cobwebs before a flame. He found that he could move somewhat.

Painfully he turned his head.

"The prisoner has recovered," observed the woman. Talon glimpsed cold, classic, austere, icy loveliness gazing dispassionately at him. At the side of this statuesque virago was a white bearded old man who leant on a staff, a glowing wand he held in his other hand. Beyond them...

They were in the middle of a large chamber. Daylight streamed in through openings in the distant roof. He stirred again and found that his movements were hampered. He was bound to a stone post, and yet the paralysis that he had felt earlier had now lifted.

"Let me go," he pleaded.

The old man-Lord Zennor?-placed the now dark wand in his belt and shuffled forwards. He peered into Talon's eyes. "When the paladin Elenara went into the catacombs to inter her slain hippogriff, you were found before an open tomb. She rescued you, slaying the arachnid that had attacked you."

"I'm very grateful." Talon gave the woman-Elenara, a pretty name-what he wrongly thought was a winning smile. Coldly she looked away. "I'm indebted to you. Now please set me free."

"You have been tried and judged while you were still unconscious," said Lord Zennor, silencing his protests with a scowl, "and your sins are deemed to be most grave. You murdered one guard, endangered the life of another-happily he is recovering in our infirmary. But those are not the worst of your crimes. Only a very evil man would rob the riches of the ancient dead."

"Oh, come on now!" said Talon. "That treasure was benefiting no one! Better I should redistribute it amongst the poor-innkeepers, brothel owners, and the seedier kind of alchemists would benefit from my generosity-than that it should spend all eternity in some underground crypt."

"You are evil," said Elenara with a snort.

"Evil?" Talon was offended. "I've done wrong in my life, but who hasn't?" His nervous laugh tailed off in the cold blaze of her withering scorn. "You don't know enough about my life, my background, to judge me. I was an orphan, living on the walkways of a floating city in the Sea of Many Islands from an early age. Even before that, life was harsh. I was beaten every day by my mother after my father ran off with another man. When my mother died in a knife fight, I ended up on the walkways. I had to steal to survive. I had no chance to make a better life for myself. But I didn't ask for this life. Lord Zennor, you"re a powerful man. You can afford to be merciful. Give me a chance and I'll change my ways, become a better person." He trailed off as Lord Zennor shook his head.

"But we want an evil man," he insisted. "We need evil to fight Evil. We have chosen you as our assassin. You will travel through the dimensions to the world of the Sons of Darkness, there to gain access to the halls of the King of Darkness. You will slay him."

Talon's face cleared. "You want me to kill someone? Well," he added with a laugh, "why didn't you say? Just set me free, point me in the right direction, and I'll set out at once. I'll need a knife."

"He'll bolt and run at the first opportunity," said Elenara, to Talon's chagrin. That was exactly what he had been considering.

Lord Zennor gave a smile. In a man less famed for his goodness of nature it might be called cruel. Even evil. With a suddenness that was almost as shocking as the action itself, he thrust out his hand and it sank impossibly into Talon's chest. The thief gasped. He thought he felt fingers clutching tightly round his heart as Lord Zennor uttered some kind of incantation.

The lord withdrew his hand, leaving no sign of any hole in Talon's chest. "A geas has been cast upon you, a sorcerous compulsion," he said. "You must fulfil this quest else die in the attempt."

"But I don't know how to travel between the dimensions," Talon carped.

"I will accompany you," Elenara said quietly. "I know the way. I will guide you to the Lands of Darkness."

"Why don't you kill its king, then?" Talon asked. "If you know how to get there."

"Evil consumes good," she droned. "Were I to set myself up against the King of Darkness, I would become evil like so many paladins who have tried before. Even if I cast him down, I would be corrupted by power, perhaps even becoming Queen of Darkness in his place. You are evil..."

"Hardly...!"

"You are evil," she insisted. "So you will be able to prevail where a paladin would fail. That is why Lord Zennor chose you as our champion."

Talon looked from the paladin to Lord Zennor in horror. All his life there had been people like this, sanctimonious, mealy mouthed hypocrites who dedicated their lives to pushing him around. None of this was fair, but he was under a sorcerous compulsion now. He had no choice. It seemed he had no option but to do as they wanted. A hopeless quest across the dimensions, just him and this lady paladin against the Forces of Darkness. There were faster ways to commit suicide.

Numbly he heard his foolish mouth say, "So when do we set out?"

SKYFALL FOREST

- Glynn Owen Barrass

As adventurers on the road, Ansell and Tamara had a knack for knowing when things were amiss. Ansell wondered if this gift for finding trouble might be a curse that dogged her. It made sense, really. She'd performed many deeds she wasn't proud of. So, when they reached the village of Kell, she received an instant bad feeling, deep in her bones. The village wasn't a surprise in itself. The sorceress Ral Pa'atha had noted it on the map she sketched for them, back in Utnar Vehi. The map also illustrated a forest beyond the village, their goal. Skyfall Forest held a fallen star, a "meteorite," the sorceress called it. Ral Pa'atha required it for some magical purpose unknown to Ansell. The sorceress paid well, this being all she needed to know.

But the village ... They had just entered the outskirts, and already it appeared quite deserted. Not unlike a village she and Tamara came across some weeks ago. That proved deserted until they discovered the corpses. Brutal, ugly deaths, caused by a winged fiend she'd met on a previous occasion. If it had come here too ... Ansell shrugged the thought off. She would deal with that if they encountered it.

"This reminds me of Vonterry," Tamara said, breaking the silence.

So she feels just the same as I do.

Her companion wore a black, hooded robe, matching her jet black hair. It contrasted greatly with the pale skin of her face and hands. The pupils of her eyes shone red. A brown leather belt around her waist held a short sword, a red leather traveling pack hung strapped to her back.

Ansell had a brown cotton bag hung over one armored shoulder. She'd return the meteorite to Utnar Vehi in it, should it fit. She also wore a sword at her hip for different encounters. Her gloved hand wavered over the sword hilt as they entered the village proper.

"Maybe there's been a storm," Tamara said. Her explanation sounded half-hearted, and the girl probably knew it.

There were no signs of a storm. The village appeared quite calm. Still, Ansell felt like circling round it, rather than pressing through.

As they walked the cobbled path, she examined the nearby buildings. A mixture of sizes, some stood one-storied, with low, hay-thatched roofs, whitewashed walls, open wooden shutters on the windows. Others stood two and three stories tall, had tiled roofs. Balconies graced many of the latter, reached by wooden steps. Not one of the multiple chimneys issued smoke. One single story house, to their left, stood fenced off and was surrounded by an artificial pool. Raised over the water on wooden stilts, barrels flanked its front door. The water looked clear, metallic slivers of fish visible flitting between the stilts.

"At least we won't go hungry," Tamara said, following her gaze.

"Locals might not like us stealing their produce," Ansell replied. "Although they may have more to worry about."

"Do you think …" Tamara shrugged. "Do you think Ral Pa'atha sent us here knowing there'd be something amiss?"

Ansell considered this for a moment. It wouldn't be the first time a patron sent her to a dangerous or deadly place.

"I don't know. News travels slowly out on this continent. Ral Pa'atha didn't even know about the Vonterry massacre, and that village is nearer to her than this."

Soon enough, they reached the village square. Beyond distant rooftops, Ansell saw the green tips of trees. The wide square boasted larger buildings than those they'd encountered so far. Some appeared to be shops, shutters closed. One was obviously an inn. "The Saucy Nancy," Ansell read from the sign. The sign held a picture of a mermaid with huge breasts. This nautical theme seemed out of place, for an inland village.

"Oh look," Tamara said, pointing right.

Ansell looked in that direction, to see a score of chickens prancing around in a pen. A large tabby and white cat sat sprawled upon a low roof behind the pen. They headed this way, Ansell feeling thankful the village wasn't completely abandoned. The chickens ignored them. Pecking away, getting along with their simple lives. The cat stood at their approach, stretched brown and black stripy legs. It yawned, its mouth revealing tiny teeth and canines, the one at the top left missing its tip. The cat sat on its haunches, scrutinized the pair with wise, green eyes.

"Hello," it said, the voice distinctly male.

"Um, hello," Tamara replied. Both she and Ansell paused before the fence.

"We were going to ask you—"

"Where all the people are?" he interrupted Tamara. "Some are hiding. Some fled. I'm surprised you didn't encounter any on the road."

Ansell and Tamara shared a glance.

The cat licked a forepaw, stopped, and continued. "Some days ago we saw flashing lights over Skyfall Forest. An almighty crashing sound came after. The braver folk entered the forest for a look. They didn't return."

"And that made the rest leave or hide?" Ansell questioned.

"The screams made the rest leave or hide," he replied.

"Oh," Ansell said, and saw Tamara grimace. Years ago, something monstrous had decimated Tamara's home village. It's how they'd first met. Perhaps the cat's words had reminded the girl of that.

Ansell thought for a moment. "Are you the only cat here?"

He nodded his large head. "The others flew away to Ulthar for a meeting. I'm keeping watch till they return."

"Thanks," Ansell said. *Well this is a pickle. Do we turn back or enter the forest?*

"If either of you make it back," the cat added, "Let me know what you find there."

This did nothing to encourage her.

"We will."

"See you," Tamara added, quietly.

The cat nodded, turned, and began cleaning his flank.

As they continued through and past the square, Ansell couldn't help but notice how distracted Tamara appeared. The houses around them, did villagers huddle behind the windows, watching them with suspicion?

"Hey, Tam, are you alright?"

Her companion frowned a moment, then, "The timescale bothers me. We left Ral Pa'atha a few days ago, on the hunt for this meteorite. I assumed it had crashed into the forest many years ago. Yet the cat said it just arrived …" She waved her hands in exasperation. "It seems odd is all. No-one in Utnar Vehi saw the light from the meteorite. We would've heard."

Tamara was correct. Unlike this nearly deserted village, nosey folk who couldn't shut up filled Utnar Vehi. If a fallen star had been witnessed, it would've reached their ears.

Ansell considered this, then replied, "Ral Pa'atha is a sorceress of great skill. Perhaps she had an omen of its arrival, or owns a scrying tool to view scenes remotely." This made sense, to her at least.

"Perhaps you're right," Tamara said. "But then wouldn't she know the village was deserted?" Her expression indicated she remained perturbed. Ansell didn't have an answer for that.

They'd reached the village outskirts now, the houses dwindled behind them, replaced by untamed grass. The cobbled path ended, though another, made of footfalls through the grass, continued to the forest. The path held cart-tracks and hoof-prints too.

The forest was a forbidding, unwelcoming sight. Too much darkness lurked between the thick, gnarly trees. Branches hung so heavy with leaves that no light entered through the canopy. The forests they'd entered in recent months had appeared far more wholesome. This one looked haunted. During her days as a hired mercenary Ansell would avoid entering the likes of this. Unless she had to. They passed the threshold into the gloom. Tamara shivered visibly. Their feet touched undergrowth patted down from footfalls. This continuance of path took a snaking route through the forest. Roots poked up where tree bark met earth, radiating around trunks like twisting tendrils. Uncomfortably face-shaped knots protruded from many trunks. Branches loomed like arms, festoons of moss hanging from them.

An unwanted thought harried Ansell: these monstrously old trees uprooting themselves to lumber towards them. Lower branches spattering moss, they'd swat her and Tamara down, breaking bones, piercing their bodies for obscene nourishment. Walking trees were things of legend. *Just like the Manticora you encountered*, another unwanted thought whispered.

"I hope this path doesn't disappear," Tamara said, disrupting her negative thought train.

Ansell dug her boot into a clod of moss, kicking it towards the trees.

"I feel like turning back already," she said halfheartedly. The sorceress Ral Pa'atha wasn't someone Ansell wanted to disappoint, however. "We'll stay the course. Find what's here to be found," she added, and sent Tamara a smile.

"Do you hear that?" Tamara asked.

"Hear what?"

"Exactly," she explained. "No birdsong from the trees. No rodents in the undergrowth. Not even a spider casting his web. This whole place is tainted. The further we go, the nearer we are to the source."

Tamara turned silent a few moments, then, "At least we know we're heading in the right direction."

That's my girl, Ansell thought. *You find light in every darkness you enter.*

"We need light," Tamara said, this one of the occasions Ansell suspected their thoughts were as bonded as their love. Tamara paused, held her left hand out palm upwards. She made movements above it with her right hand. A moment later, a small ball of illumination materialized in the air.

The light moved ahead as they continued down the path of disturbed undergrowth. A welcome companion, it dispersed many shadows. Ansell felt safer as a result.

As they progressed, Ansell noted small lumps of fungi clinging to tree roots. Some were the color of flesh, others: bone white. The deeper they breached the forest, the more abundant the parasitic fungi became. White clumps clung to branches, bulged from gaps between roots. Fat yellow toadstools ribbed some trunks in uneven, ascending patterns. With the fungi came a foul smell, ripe and rotten. It made Ansell's back itch beneath her armor.

"If I were a better herbalist, I could probably find some use for this fungus," Tamara said.

Ansell grunted assent. Larger heaps of white fungus spotted the undergrowth now. They made half-familiar shapes she didn't like the look of. Some distance ahead, a gap in the leafy ceiling brought light to the forest. Tiny motes there danced through the air. By the complex way they maneuvered one another their movements appeared choreographed.

"The smell's getting worse," Tamara said. She paused,

removed the pack from her shoulders and knelt. "Those spores, exposed by the daylight," she continued, rooting through the bag, "I'd rather not breathe them in."

Ansell knelt, observed the concentration on her companion's face.

Tamara, retrieving a green shawl from her sack, proceeded to rip it in two. "We put these around our faces," she explained. "It'll hinder us breathing in the spores." Tamara wrapped the shawl around her face, tying the ends up behind her head. She stood, re-shouldered her pack, and handed the other piece of shawl to Ansell, who placed the fabric over her face, tying it like her companion had. They continued into the gloom, Tamara's globe of light moving a short distance before them.

Another break in the forest canopy lay ahead. Something from the sky had broken branches in its descent to the forest. In an area of dark browns and the ever-present fungi, the large yellow object stood out clearly.

Perhaps it wants to be found, Ansell thought uneasily.

"Is this the meteorite?" Tamara asked. Her voice sounded a little muffled from the mask.

"I guess so."

Daylight from the open canopy revealed air filled with spores. White fungus grew thickly around the object's base. The trodden path became an area of disturbed moss and leaf matter. They paused as one. To Ansell's experienced gaze, it appeared as though some fight or struggle had occurred here. No bodies though. No sign of who, or what, had caused it.

Tamara continued forward, Ansell following till they halted before the crash site. The object, twice as tall as a man, resembled a giant yellow seed pod.

"How did the fungus grow so quickly, if this only dropped from the sky a few days ago?" Tamara shrugged.

A good question. One she didn't have an answer for. Ansell silently scrutinized the pod. A circular portal stood near the top, formed of glass too dark to see through. Their companion light reflected off it.

"I don't like this," Tamara said quietly. She made a hand movement across her chest. A blessing against evil, Ansell guessed.

Ansell looked to the girl, then the pod. Her companion held a close link to the mysterious, the mystical. Hence she asked: "What can you sense?"

Tamara went to step closer, paused in indecision. "Don't like it. Can't stand it. There's something so ... forbidden about the thing."

Unable to feel what Tamara did, Ansell trusted the girl's instincts. "Will it harm me though. Trigger some kind of magical trap if I attempt to open it?"

"No. It's not magical in nature," Tamara replied. "Just ... wrong."

Ansell steeled herself and stepped forward. Up close, she discovered the object was constructed from metal. Rather than having a smooth surface, segmented sections were pieced together with circular bolts. She noted something beneath the upper fungus, some other colors; reaching over, she began clearing it away, thankful that her hands were gloved.

"I think something's watching us," Tamara said, a tremble in her voice. "One thing, yet all around us."

Ansell paused her scraping, looked around. She examined the hulking, bent trees, the bulging humps of fungi. "Stay vigilant, and let me know if anything changes."

She returned to her task. The growths she sent to her feet revealed a strange image. Rectangular, formed of alternating lines, red, then white. She found more to it as she cleared the area to the left. A blue square inside the rectangle, spotted in tiny white stars.

Interesting, she thought, starting on the area beneath the rectangle.

More markings came uncovered, this time glyphs in a language she half-recognized. Tamara stepped closer, brushing past Ansell as she leant forward.

"It's reminiscent of a tongue they use in Celephaïs. Very similar." Tamara touched the surface with bare, delicate fingers. "NASA X-38," she said slowly.

The word was alien to Ansell. Tamara stepped back. "Let's look inside."

"You sure?"

Tamara ignored her companion. She stepped around the pod, disappearing from view. The ball of light went with her. Ansell shook her head, returned to fungus removal.

"Trees are a little burned on this side," Tamara said. "Come look."

"In a moment." She'd found something new: a circular indentation with a red handle at its center. Ansell gripped the handle, tried to give it a turn. It shifted a little in her hand.

Tamara's enthusiasm to open the pod appeared contagious. Reaching for a tree trunk for support, she tugged again, with no better result. She went to twist the handle clockwise. It started to turn.

The forest exploded with noise: loud popping sounds filling the air from every direction. Ansell ceased what she was doing and spun round. The large humps of fungus had burst open, disgorging man-like forms. Clouds of spores surrounded them as they stood and lurched forward.

"What the?" *The missing villagers?* Ansell guessed, or they had been villagers, at some point.

"Are you seeing this?" Tamara shouted from the other side of the pod.

"Hard to miss," Ansell replied. Unsheathing her sword, she gripped it two-handed, taking up a fighter's stance. The approaching things came slowly, interminably, stepping around trees and stumbling as they walked. Dressed in the barest tatters of clothes, the travesties of men moved in silence. Parts of their bodies were bloated with fungus. Others were eaten away, ribs and organs protruding beneath half-consumed flesh. The nearest one had bare skull on one side of its face, the other ripe with fungus. A staring, misshapen eye bulged from the puffy mass. Half alive, half dead, still it came forward, with malefic intent.

Tamara rushed to her side. "We're surrounded," she gasped.

We're screwed, Ansell thought.

"You got enough juice to take them down?"

"There must be fifty of them. I just don't know," the girl replied

Tamara raised her hands, stuffed fingers in her mouth. She whistled loudly. The ball of light sped into view, paused to hover before them. Tamara flung a hand in the direction of a villager. The ball darted towards him, the impact engulfing him in flame. The man struggled weakly. He dropped to his knees, then his face, still burning. Despite her mask, the acrid scent of smoldering flesh filled Ansell's nostrils. Tamara invoked another ball of light, then another, attacking the walking horrors with each. Ansell maintained her fighter's stance, watched warily as the villagers made their slow approach.

Can we force our way through them, me in the lead? The villagers appeared fairly fragile. But if they weren't? Skull-face stumbled within striking distance. Ansell lunged, impaling him through his rotten chest. Her assault achieved naught. The dead villager, for surely these were all animated corpses, waved his arms and attempted to grab her. She rammed her boot into his chest, sent him flailing back as she withdrew the sword.

So they don't die like real men.

She turned to Tamara. The girl appeared fatigued already, despite having immolated only half dozen of their attackers. The one she'd knocked down started climbing up, that hideous, bulging eye still staring. Ansell swung her sword, lopped his head clean off. His decapitated body continued to rise.

Ansell's eyes began to water from the fetid smoke. She blinked away tears. Looking around in exasperation, she realized they were completely surrounded. Her panicked gaze locked on the pod's handle. The villagers only appeared when she'd tried opening it. *What if ...*

"Hold out just a little longer," she said before rushing back to the pod.

What if what's inside is the key to this?

She slammed her sword into the earth, reached for the red handle. For a moment, it seemed it wouldn't give. Ansell gasped in relief when it turned. A hiss filled the air. Thick white gas erupted from the pod. The pod's top detached, sliding up like a trapdoor. The gas dissipated quickly, revealing the interior.

"Ansell, they've stopped," Tamara said with hope in her voice.

She wanted to reply, but stood quietly awed by what she'd discovered. The pod's interior held a body strapped to a red fabric chair. It wore the strangest armor Ansell had ever seen. Constructed from grey metallic plates and white cloth padding, its shoulder plates bore the same stars and stripes as the pod's exterior. The helmet, a large globe of mirrored glass, reflected her panicked face. Flesh-colored roots, spotted in white fungus, had infesting the pod, entering the body in multiple places. Ansell flinched as Tamara's hand touched her shoulder.

"They're just stood there," she said.

Ansell looked round, saw the corpses close but frozen in place. Their rotted and bloated arms remained outstretched towards them. "What do we do," Ansell hissed. "Burn it?"

If the dead men continued forward, they'd be engulfed.

"That body there, it's connected to the forest," Tamara whispered.

Connected, Ansell thought. "Start pulling away the roots, fast as you can," she replied." I'll try getting the body from the chair."

Tamara dashed forward, began ripping away tangles of

root matter from around the prone form. A brown liquid oozed from the disconnection points. Ansell smelled something sour and organic through her mask. She went for the straps, found them strong and unyielding.

"They're moving again," Tamara hissed, panic in her voice.

Ansell grasped the triangular object the straps fed into. A red button stood at the center. Brown gore spattered her arm.

"Sorry," Tamara said.

Ansell heard closing footsteps. She jabbed the button, and the straps across the body's shoulders detached. *Dammit.* The strap around the waist felt loose, but would not budge. A fungus-caked hand reached for her. She shoved it away.

"Grab the legs!" Tamara yelled.

The legs, of course. Ansell gripped the right leg, her companion, the left. They pulled with all their might. The body snapped away from the remaining roots as they tugged it from the seat. Brown ooze poured. Ansell dared a look around. The walking corpses walked no longer. They had fallen as one. She encountered an obstruction: the bulbous helmet wouldn't move past the strap. It didn't matter now. All the roots were severed, dripping ichor into the pod. Ansell released the leg, wiped her sweaty brow.

They backed off, turned to examine the aftermath of the attack. The forest floor lay littered with corpses, the undergrowth barely visible beneath decomposed flesh and moldy protuberances. The still-smoldering bodies Tamara had dispatched lay twisted and crisp. Ansell went to retrieve her sword. A corpse's arm crunched horribly under her foot.

"We ought to burn these things." Tamara giggled nervously. "With flint and steel 'cos I'm all worn out."

Shrugging a knot out of her shoulder, Ansell replied. "No. Let's just leave them, they're the villagers problem, not ours."

Tamara nodded, turned back to the pod. "So this ... vehicle, brought the fungus with it?"

"Perhaps," Ansell said, and moved to Tamara's side. "Or maybe it reacted with the fungus here, turned it bad. They were certainly linked."

"And it came from up there, eh?" Tamara said.

Ansell looked past the break in the trees to the sky. Whatever mysteries lurked up there, she hoped they'd remain as such.

The village stood just as empty as before. The cat even sat in the same spot near the chickens. They informed him what had occurred. He took the news without surprise, appeared unperturbed by the near wholesale decimation of the villagers. He thanked them for their service, offered a couple of chickens should they wish to remain in the village to cook them. They were hungry, but not enough to stay longer than needed in that doomed, desolate place.

After searching the square they discovered a cart and a domesticated yak to move it. Returning to the forest, and after some work and a lot of cursing, they succeeded in lifting the pod onto the cart. They rode a circuitous route around Kell. Ansell didn't intend to give the beast and cart back, or pay for them for that matter.

A slow, uneventful journey to Utnar Vei returned them to Ral Pa'atha's castle. They gained quite a following of curious locals on the way. These they left at the castle gate. It turned out that the meteorite Ral Pa'atha wanted was a rock around the size of cow's head. They'd retrieved the wrong object, the pod being as much as a mystery to the sorceress as it was to Ansell and Tamara. Ral Pa'atha's anger changed to curiosity when they described the incident in the forest.

And as always, the sorceress paid well...

SKYFALL FOREST

THE GUIDE, THE GENERAL AND THE PRIEST

- Shelley De Cruz

"**A** sorcerer? I've no time for sorcerers!" The man opposite spat onto the rush-strewn floor and took another swig of the dark liquid in his mug.

General Sangyal swiftly pulled back his polished boots and brushed a speck of dirt from his silk sleeve. "With respect, Tehmjin, what you do or do not like is not the issue here. Can you guide us across the hills and through the swampland beyond? That is all that is required of you."

He grimaced as the man belched and wiped his mouth with the back of his hand. Tehmjin was not a tall man, but was powerfully built. His black hair hung in a single long braid, green eyes glittered in an angular face, the skin bronzed by the winds of the steppe. By all accounts he was the best guide in this area, a true man of the wilds, raised in the saddle as was the way of his people. The General continued.

"The Yellow Priest has charged me with investigating reports of sorcerous activities to the north."

Tehmjin scowled. "First a sorcerer, and now a priest? Ancestors preserve us!" His eyes flickered towards the General's cup. "Are you not finishing your drink?"

Sangyal glanced down at the dubious contents of his mug and slid it across the table. "The Yellow Priest is no mere preacher. He is the true ruler of Yarlung, the Great Khalsang, Master of the Order of Lheng." He repressed a shudder. Even here, in the far northern reaches of Yarlung, it did not do to speak openly about the Yellow Priest. Sangyal thought back to the summons he had received; the audience in the incense-filled chamber; the saffron robed figure on the strangely wrought throne; the thin, papery voice that issued from the blank, silk mask. None had ever seen behind that mask. It was said to do so invited madness and death. The thud of an emptied mug on the table brought him back to the present. He changed tack.

"You'll be well paid. Three zho a day, plus a bonus of ten zho on our return here."

Tehmjin considered the offer. "You're very young to be a General, aren't you? Very well, but make the bonus twenty."

Sangyal nodded. He was a warrior, not a haggling trader. "Twenty it is. We ride at dawn."

"Time for more drinks, then." The guide gave a wolfish grin. "You're paying."

***

Tehmjin pulled on his boots, splashed water on his face, brushed straw from his hair, and tried to ignore the pounding in his temples. Curse these military types and their early morning starts. A rooster crowed as he prepared his horse for the journey. The stocky beast stood patiently as the high-ridged saddle was positioned, the curved hunting bow and plain leather quiver hung from it. A rolled pack slung behind carried what little gear Tehmjin required. That done, he tightened the belt holding his saber and long knife, picked up his fur-trimmed helm and led the horse out into the crisp, morning air. Sangyal and his troop were ready and waiting. The General sat ramrod straight in the saddle of his fine mount, his dark, lacquered armour shining in the dawn rays. The red silk of his sleeves matched not only his cloak but also the horse-hair plume that hung from the peak of the conical helm tucked under his arm. Young, yes, but the close-cropped hair and stern features spoke of an inner discipline, Tehmjin thought. Not a man to be trifled with.

About the General sat his unit, ten mounted men in similar garb, all armed with the heavy, curved *dao* typical of Yarlung soldiery. Amongst them sat another rider, this one in a thin, yellow robe, shaven headed, older than his companions. Despite the thin garment he showed no sign of noticing the cold. Tehmjin walked his mount across and nodded.

"Morning, General," he offered.

"Morning, Tehmjin? Well it still is, just about." The General placed the helm on his head. "I wanted us to have left by now!"

Tehmjin left the rebuke hanging and mounted his horse. There was snigger from the ranks. The steppe-man's eyes flashed at the sound.

"Who was that?"

One of the soldiers nudged his powerful horse forward. "It was I. You aim to guide us on this... this pony? How will you keep up?" The remark brought a ripple of laughter from his comrades.

In the blink of an eye Tehmjin leapt his horse alongside the fellow, whipped out his saber and rested the point on the notch of the soldier's throat.

"In my land," he hissed, "To insult a man's horse is to insult his honour, his family and his clan. Men have died for less."

Sangyal pushed his own horse between the two. "Come, Tehmjin, it was a mere jest nothing more. Let us not begin our journey in anger. Lhatse, apologise for your rudeness to our guide. Besides, you display double ignorance, for all know that the steeds of the steppe warriors are the hardiest of all breeds."

Apologies mumbled, honour restored, the group set off up the narrow trail that snaked from the inn towards the lower slopes of the grey hill range dominating the skyline. Tehmjin led and, after a time, the General drew his horse alongside.

"Apologies for my men. Few of them have ever left the Imperial Palace."

"You are Royal Guard, then?" Tehmjin raised an eyebrow. "I should be honoured." To himself he was thinking that the presence of such elite troops spoke of more than a casual reconnaissance. There may well be loot to be had from this venture. Outwardly he asked, "And the old man in the robes?"

"A priest," came the reply. "An adept of the Order. Sent to assist us, if need be. And no doubt keep an eye on us," he added beneath his breath.

***

For three days they saw no-one save a solitary goat-herd and his bleating flock. There was little trade in this area, so no major routes, but Tehmjin knew the local trails well. At night they huddled in cloaks around small fires. None of the soldiers spoke to Tehmjin, which was fine by him.

He noticed the priest also sat alone, chanting softly to himself, or occasionally tittering in a most unnerving way. On the morning of the fourth day they began to descend, riding through terraced fields, beyond which lay a large village. Toilers looked up at their passing and a boy ran off ahead of the group. By the time they reached the outskirts of the village, a woman, flanked by two men carrying spears was coming to meet them. Tehmjin noticed other villagers lurking amongst the buildings, bows at the ready.

The woman, middle-aged and sturdily built, stood hands on hips at their approach, scowling, one hand resting on her knife hilt. Sangyal drew level with Tehmjin and called a halt.

"I'd have thought they'd send their Chief out to greet us," the General muttered.

"She is their Chief, you idiot. She is Mother to the clan." Tehmjin slipped easily from the saddle and strode towards the trio, a grin on his face.

"Ho, Mother. Don't you recognise a friend?" He spoke in the local dialect.

The woman's scowl faded. "Young Tehmjin, you rascal! We've not seen you for many a moon. What brings you here and who are these people? Why does this one ride like he has a pole up his backside?"

"Just some people I'm guiding through the wilds,"

Tehmjin replied.

Sangyal spurred his horse forward, proclaiming loudly, "I am General Sangyal of the Imperial Guard, representative of His Imperial Highness. I am on a mission for the High and Holy Khalsang, the Yellow Priest. You shall afford us a night's hospitality."

Mother's eyebrows arched. She muttered to Tehmjin, "His Imperial Highness can kiss my arse. But if this boy and his soldiers are with you, I suppose they can stay."

"What does she say?" called the General.

"She says you look like a magnificent warrior, and all praise be to our glorious ruler," the guide responded. "Tell the men to dismount, we bed here over-night."

Later, the guide, the general, and the priest sat cross-legged at Mother's low table, enjoying bowls of hot stew. Tehmjin explained the purpose of the expedition but at mention of the swamp, Mother's face dropped again.

"The swamp, eh? We avoid it now. Time was we used to fish and hunt there. But hunters went out and never returned. Worse still, many of those who lived near the edges of the swamp disappeared. The place has changed. It's evil. Don't go there."

Tehmjin translated to Sangyal who shrugged. "Peasant superstition. We have a troop of Imperial Guard, we'll not be deterred by local gossip."

Mother was speaking again. "A sorcerer, some say. Beyond the swamp stands an old fortress. Back from the time when his people," she jutted her chin towards the General, "lorded it over these lands."

The steppe-man stared into the flickering flames of the peat fire. "I don't like it any more than you, Mother. But they are paying me, I've agreed, and so across the swamp we go."

"If you must go, then take this." She rummaged in her jacket and handed over a thin chain. Tehmjin held it up, spinning slowly, glinting in the fire glow. It was a small amulet in the shape of an eye, a symbol of Ulga the All-seeing. Inwardly he groaned. He had no time for gods or trinkets. Outwardly he bowed his thanks, tucking the charm into an inside pocket. Then he lifted his empty mug.

"Is there any more ale?"

**

At noon the next day, they reached the swamp edge. The slopes were behind them, before lay a hazy green-brown smudge that extended to the far horizon. The air grew warm and humid, worse were the insects. By the time they rode into the marsh proper, the blood-suckers were swarming around all - save the enigmatic priest. Tehmjin was ill at ease. Although he knew the trails here, his natural environment was the open steppe, where a man might see the approach of an enemy. Here, anyone or anything might be lurking amongst the tall reeds and shadowed thickets. Yet the day and night passed without event. It was the next morning that death struck.

The group were readying to move off. Kicking over the small fire at the centre of the hillock they'd spent the night on; tightening tack, pissing into the reeds, rolling up blankets. An arrowhead of geese honked overhead in the pale dawn air. Tehmjin was talking quietly to his horse when he heard the sounds - a slap of water, an unfinished scream and a splash. In an instant he was across the clearing, blade in hand. One of the soldiers was gone, the only sign of his passing a lessening stream of bubbles and emerald undulations across the stagnant mere. Sangyal was at his side.

"By the gods! What was it?"

"I didn't see. It must have been big to take a fully armoured man in one go. We should leave."

Behind, the horses were already whinnying in unease. The General nodded and barked terse orders. Within minutes the group were along the trail, the soldiers now nervously glancing around at each step.

At the first touch, Sangyal was awake. He grabbed the wrist of the touching hand, and reached for the sword at his side. Tehmjin's face was a soft blur above him in the glow of the camp fire.

"The sentry is gone," hissed the guide. Sangyal sprang up, alert. Tehmjin was peering into the darkness beyond the circle of light. At dusk they had camped on a mound almost at the far edge of the swamp. All was silent. Too silent; the night air was usually filled with the buzz of insects, the splash of hunting creatures. Now, silence lay as heavy as the curiously green-tinged fog that swirled around their knees. The soldiers were indistinct shapes in the gloom, stirring from their slumber.

"There!" Tehmjin pointed with his saber. A wan face floated in the dark. Then more, one to each side of it. Pallid, sickly of complexion, hair lank, lips slack and drooling. Their eyes glistened, wet and white.

"Who are you? What do you want?" Sangyal demanded. "You face an officer of the Imperial Court!"

There came no answer, other than a pulling back of the lips, revealing the stumps of blackened teeth.

"More behind!" warned a soldier, then the three in front surged forward, mottled hands raised.

The General met the attack, kicking out at the first figure, slicing down with his sword as it was knocked back. The blade sank deep into the shoulder, snapping the collarbone like a twig. A dark, viscous fluid oozed from the wound, yet the thing struck out, dealing Sangyal a backhand blow with its other hand. As he fell back, Sangyal saw Tehmjin lunge forward, impaling the second attacker on his point. The thing did not slow its advance, it pushed forward up the blade, cupping the guide's head between outstretched hands.

Sangyal rolled out of the fall, ears ringing, and was up on his feet in an instant. Around him, silhouettes closed and grappled in the dim orange glow. The attackers were silent and Sangyal became aware of their stench now, the stench of things long left rotting in the sludge. He kicked out again, then dropped and span, sweeping his attacker's legs out from under him. As he had done so many times in training, he followed with a downward thrust to pin his opponent to the ground. The thing on the floor merely grinned up at him, sliding hands up the blade to grab at his arm. With a savage yank, the General pulled back, yelling, "By the gods! These things are not human!"

"Cripple them," Tehmjin cried. He had drawn his long knife and all but severed his attacker's hands. "Cut their strings!" As he shouted he dropped, viciously slicing behind his foe's knee and ankle. The thing staggered awkwardly, stumbling to fall heavily onto the fire. The smell of singed flesh mingled with the foetid swamp odour.

Sangyal decided on a different course. His heavy curved blade was not designed for delicate slicing. With a shout he brought the blade down in two heavy blows, severing the legs of the creature below him. More liquid oozed, the smell worsened. With a final cut, the General struck off the thing's head and turned to aid his men. Five more shapes were tearing and biting at them, one sinking its rotten teeth into the neck of a guard. Sangyal cut it down in two blows, cleaving limb and spine. The thing flopped at his feet, mouth shiny with fresh blood. Tehmjin streaked past, saber a whistling blur, sending another figure to the ground.

"Cover your eyes!" came a shout from the priest. Sangyal threw an arm across his face. Another shout, a loud whoosh and a feeling of intense heat. Daring to look again, he caught the afterglow of a huge flash. The attackers were staggering back blindly, hair and the rags they wore smouldering. Within seconds the soldiers cut them into pieces. Sangyal grimaced as hands and other body parts wriggled on the ground. Kicking a writhing arm away into the swamp, he turned to take stock. The sentry was gone, two others lay still on the ground. The man who had been bitten knelt, hand pressed to neck, eyes wide in pain and fear.

"Well that was interesting." Tehmjin was wiping his blade clean on a tussock.

"I take it you never saw those when you were here before?"

"New to me. Still, your pet priest helped. Though in doing so he alerted any watchers in the area to our presence."

Sangyal said nothing. Four men dead already and they had yet to meet this sorcerer. Would any of them return from this cursed mission?

***

The man who had been bitten died at dawn, screaming, face horribly discoloured and contorted. Sangyal ordered the body cremated. To the relief of all they came out of the swamp late next afternoon. Climbing a steep gradient brought them to a point overlooking a valley, a river at its centre. On the high ridge opposite perched the squat outline of a fortress, its walls blood red in the dipping sun. Tehmjin sniffed the clean air with appreciation. Some leagues beyond that ridge lay the steppe, his homeland. It called to him as ever. His horse, perhaps sensing the same, shook her mane and whinnied. He patted her neck and turned to the General.

"There's a narrow trail leads down. We can pick up that road, there. See? A bridge crosses the river. It does mean we approach the fortress in the open, though."

Sangyal stroked his chin. "The fortress looks long abandoned. We've had no forces stationed here in my lifetime. We will take the road, direct is best. The men are spooked enough, I'll not prolong this expedition any more than need be."

Tehmjin shrugged. Not his plan, but then he wasn't a General. With a click he nudged his mount down the slope. The road was wide and dusty, unused and in poor repair. The river was slow and sluggish and in places gleamed with a peculiar green tinge. It flowed from a place by the fortress above, then away into the swamp. The guide cast his eyes towards the bridge ahead. A large, single arched stone structure, it appeared clear and open. So why was something tingling at the back of his neck? Sangyal obviously felt the same, as he called a halt, motioning one of his men to dismount and investigate. The soldier slid to the ground, pebbles crunching under his boots as he strode towards the bridge, sword in hand. He stood at its threshold glancing around, and slowly stepped across. He paused halfway, sniffing the air, then turned to his colleagues.

"Seems safe, General," he called and retraced his steps. As he stepped back onto the road, a shape from hell struck.

From beneath the bridge it scuttled on many legs, a glistening, chitinous shape, claws waving. Before the soldier had a chance to move, it was on him, the stinger on its curved tail stabbing violently between the man's shoulder blades. He gave a hoarse scream as the massive scorpion scooped him up in one claw, his lips already turning blue, eyes rolling back in their sockets. Another scuttle, and the creature was gone, back below the bridge, the soldier's sword the only sign that he had ever been there.

Tehmjin cursed, Sangyal was slack-jawed, even the priest look shocked. The horses picked up on the panic, whickering and backing off. The General set his jaw and span to face his troop.

"Control yourselves! Control your mounts! You are men of the Imperial Guard, stand firm!"

Discipline re-asserted, the group moved back a little from

the bridge to assess the situation.

Sangyal thought for a while, then announced the plan. It was not to Tehmjin's liking. As they now had spare horses, the plan was to use one of them to lure the creature back out into the open. That would hopefully leave an opening for them to charge across the bridge. In Tehmjin's mind a good horse was as valuable as a good warrior - to sacrifice one in such a way was unthinkable. Muttering, he unslung the short, curved bow, selecting three heavy, barbed arrows from his quiver.

"Ready your men," he called to Sangyal. "I'll deal with that thing."

Before the General could respond, the guide was off away towards the bridge, hooves pounding in the dust. He trotted onto the bridge, turned and cantered back. The scorpion, obviously not satisfied with its previous morsel, shot forth again, but this time its prey was ready.

"Go!" Tehmjin shouted to the troop. "Go, now!" as he wheeled his mount away along the river bank. The beast followed, moving at speed, pincers clacking, stinger dripping venom. It drew close and struck out but Tehmjin's horse was quicker. With a deft twist it span almost on the spot and its rider put an arrow into the horror below. It hit, but skittered into the dust, the thing's shiny jet hide was like plate armour! With a wild cry Tehmjin urged his mount away, skipping it sideways to dodge the sweep of a claw. The next arrow was already strung and as he rode away, Tehmjin twisted in the saddle to release his second shot. This one hit a front eye, knocking the scorpion off course for an instant.

Beyond, Tehmjin saw the troop galloping across the

bridge, safely to the far bank. He veered away from the river, drawing the beast with him, before pulling up his mount with a sharp turn. One arrow left. He spat and gave a loud cry, urging his mount into a charge, this time directly towards the clacking nightmare. Keeping to the side of the damaged eye, he headed at the beast, veering aside at the last minute. The tail lashed out, splashing hot venom on his face as it flashed past. Tehmjin rose in his stirrups, aimed directly down, and fired the hunting arrow point blank into the thing's head. The barbs bit deep and the creature began thrashing, as though desperately trying to remove the source of its agony.

The steppe-man didn't wait to see if it succeeded, he pointed his horse back towards the bridge and was quickly back amongst the wide-eyed troop.

"By the gods," Sangyal exclaimed. "I've heard you steppe riders could shoot from the saddle, but never have I seen such a display! Well done, man, you saved us all!"

Tehmjin merely grunted in response, his people were not given to flattery. "It is I who should thank you," he responded. "I knew I could escape the thing. I was more concerned that there might be another beast at this end of the bridge too. You were the bait." He laughed at Sangyal's expression, then clicked his mount onwards up the road towards the fortress.

As they rode up the slope, they happened upon a small dell set amidst a grove of stunted trees a short distance from the road.

"We camp here for the night," ordered the General. "We ride to the fortress at dawn."

"With respect, General," Tehmjin spoke as the men dismounted and began making camp, "Might it be better to use the cover of darkness to approach the fortress? After all, one does not simply stride into a sorcerer's lair."

Sangyal fixed the feedbag to his horse as he replied. "Yes, you may be right. Very well, we shall leave a man here with the horses and push ahead on foot once we are rested."

This time a pair of sentries were posted, only a small fire lit. As they sat chewing tough strips of meat, Sangyal continued his earlier praise of Tehmjin's feat. The guide, uncomfortable with the plaudits, thought it only polite to respond in kind.

"But your movements, General, back there in the swamp. Most interesting. Those kicks!"

Sangyal shrugged. "I fight as I was taught. From the age of five I was taken into the Imperial Court, along with many others and trained in the arts of war."

"Tough training?"

"It was certainly.... arduous." Sangyal thought back to long hours of excruciating stances, the rolling and tumbling, the iron discipline, the beatings. "And you? You must have practiced hard to be so skilled?"

Tehmjin swigged on his water flask. "Me? No, I never practiced much at all."

Sangyal was aghast. "Never practiced? But how...?"

Tehmjin wrapped his blanket around his shoulders and rolled onto his side. "Never had time to practice. Too busy fighting. Wake me when it's time to leave."

***

The fortress walls loomed forbiddingly in the pre-dawn light. Tehmjin glided soundlessly over the rocky terrain. After him came the General, the priest and four soldiers. One guard remained with the horses. Tehmjin signaling a halt, vanished into the darkness of the outer wall. Soon came a low whistle. The troop moved up to where the guide crouched amongst the boulders.

"I've scouted the perimeter," he whispered. "The main gateway is closed but there are gaps in the walls. See, here? The place looks to be in disrepair. Fortunate for us."

Sangyal nodded. "Lead on. Let us hope we find this wizard abed."

Before they could move, the priest clutched at the General's arm. "It is time I told you why I am here," he croaked. "This sorcerer purloined a certain tome from the Order. A grimoire most ancient and precious, one that it is vital we recover. Such is the Great Khalsang's command to me."

"Stolen from the Order? But how would...?" Sangyal replied, before understanding dawned in his eyes. "Ah. He is one of your own, then? A renegade!"

The priest's eyes flashed in the faint light. "The affairs of the Order are of no concern to the likes of you. You shall do all you can to assist in the return of the book. That is all!"

Tehmjin stifled a laugh. It seemed that even Generals could be outranked. Sangyal, lips pressed with fury, turned back to the guide, hissing, "Lead on, man, lead on."

Part of the wall had crumbled, leaving a pile of rubble to clamber up. The group moved slowly, pausing at any noise of sliding stone to listen. No alarm was sounded and, as dawn fully bloomed, the deserted interior of the fortress was slowly revealed. It was a standard Imperial outpost of the kind found on every border of Yarlung. Outer walls, a square central keep, a handful of outbuildings and a well, built to house a few troops of soldiers. Tehmjin nudged the General and pointed up. A light could be seen flickering in a narrow, upper window of the keep. In turn, the group slid down to the packed dirt floor and drifted like ghosts across to the keep. Blades were drawn as they circled round to the entrance, an arch filled with a thick, wooden door. Tehmjin reached out and the heavy portal moved slightly under his cautious palm. He poked his head through the gap.

The shadowy interior revealed no danger, and the troop followed the guide in to a sparsely furnished chamber. The priest was quietly muttering to himself, some kind of charm or ward, perhaps. A central staircase rose up, flanked by a handful of doors and dark archways. Tehmjin slipped around the table and chairs to place a foot on the first step, straining eyes and ears upward. Sangyal beckoned two men to check the archways. One of them, Lhatse, reported back, "Stairs leading down, General. I heard movement down there."

The General nodded and signaled Lhatse to stay and guard the upper approach. The rest of the men he bade follow him, one of them lighting a brand to illumine their way.

The stone steps wound down into a small chamber, from which led a passageway. Low moans drifted out from the gloom, pulling the group onwards. Along the passageway were a number of barred cells. Some were empty, some contained the source of the moans. Villagers, from the look of them, in various states of distress and despair. Some did not even glance up at the flickering light. One, however, cursed at their approach.

"Are you here again, you devil? Come to take more of us for your foul purposes? Step closer and I'll give you something to remember. I'll gouge your eyes, you son of a dog!" Tehmjin grinned as the invective continued, growing ever more inventive and coarse. The torch-glow revealed a woman tightly gripping the bars ahead as she spat defiance.

"Easy, sister," called Tehmjin. "We are soldiers, here to help. You are one of Mother's people?"

"Aye, I am. My name is Yisu," replied the woman. She was perhaps twenty years of age, long black hair straggled across her thin face. "We lived by the swamp. Things came and took us. And every now and then the swine above comes down and takes a few of us away." She gasped at the appearance of the priest from the gloom. "He looks like him! Curse you, you said you were here to help!"

Tehmjin raised a palm. "All is well, Yisu. This is a tame one. It seems the one upstairs has fled from their Order, this one is here to punish him, or return him, or something. But let's get you people out."

Each of the cells had a lock, but they were crude and Tehmjin had spent time thieving in the cities. Before long, all the prisoners were freed, though some needed aid to stand. The General took charge as the group returned to the entrance chamber.

"Tehmjin, tell her to lead these people to go down to our guard and horses. They can wait there. If we don't return by the time the sun is high, they can take the horses and return to their homes as best they can."

Yisu began quietly giving instructions to the other prisoners. They nodded and began to leave. Yisu stayed. Sangyal glanced questioningly at her, Tehmjin explained.

"She wishes to extract vengeance on the sorcerer. Most of her family disappeared upstairs. I'll not stop her, in fact, I've given her my knife."

The General shook his head. "A woman fighting alongside the Imperial Guard?"

Tehmjin laughed. "Welcome to the real world, General. Out here, all fight for survival. I'll wager she's a match for any of your men."

"Very well, but tell her to keep out of the way. Now, let us try upstairs. We've made enough noise to wake the dead."

The General led the group slowly up the steps. Three floors they trod, passing empty barrack rooms, and other chambers. At the top of the uppermost flight stood a closed door. Sangyal turned to the priest.

"Well, what do you advise?"

"In and quick," replied the shaven headed cleric. "Give him no time to unleash a spell. I may be able to counter anything he does, but at times even mindless brawn can overcome wit."

Sangyal nodded and whispered orders before, on a count of three, crashing through the door and into the sorcerer's lair.

The entire upper floor of the keep had been opened up into one large chamber. Dark hangings covered the stone wall, what appeared to be corpses reposed on a number of slabs. Two large tables were covered in various, vials, flasks and alembics. A large vat in the corner emitted the same coruscant green they had seen in swamp and river. Two figures turned at the crash. One, a hulking brute dressed in a dark robe, a butcher's cleaver at his belt. The other stood at a lectern on which rested a heavy tome. This one, thin, shaven headed, raised a scarlet-robed arm at the intrusion.

"Choden!" shouted the priest, pushing his way through the doorway. "I am here to serve the will of the Holy Khalsang!"

The heavy set man was already advancing, cleaver raised. Sangyal moved to intercept him. Choden laughed and flung his hands outwards.

"Jinpa, you spineless fool! You think your Yellow Priest holds any authority here?"

One of the soldiers charged at the wizard, Jinpa shouted a warning. "No! Do not enter his circle of power, he -"

The warning was cut short as a sickly violet ray sprung forth from Choden's curved fingers. It enveloped the soldier and he screamed in terror as his flesh melted away. By the time he hit the floor, little more than bones remained.

Sangyal checked his forward rush in time; no matter, the brute was coming to him. He dodged the first swing of the cleaver, lashing out at the man's ribs. The assistant was quick though, far quicker than his bulk would suggest. He twisted, slicing up with the heavy blade, cutting the General's forearm. Sangyal gave no indication of the pain, nor did the wound slow him. Tossing his sword to his left hand he chopped down into the side of his foe's leg with a sickening crunch, bringing the brute down to one knee, snarling face now slack with shock. Without pause, the General span, taking the man's head clean off with one slice.

Tehmjin had also been about to rush the sorcerer when,

he too, heeded the priest's warning. Now he could see the circle on the floor, a finger-width line edged with sorcerous sigils. He cursed the fact that his bow remained on his horse and instead prowled the circumference of the circle like a wolf circling its prey.

The saffron-robed Jinpa was gesturing now, face creased in concentration. There appeared to be a battle of wills going on. At first, the priest looked to have the upper hand, but Choden placed a hand on the book, as if drawing unholy strength from it. For a time the pair were evenly matched... then a thin tickle of blood ran from Jinpa's nose. His hands began shaking, a tremor that spread throughout his whole body. Now blood also ran from his eyes and ears until, with a final cry and gesture from the sorcerer, the priest's body appeared to fold in on itself. There sounded the sickening snap of bone, the grind and crunch of joints unnaturally twisted, and Jinpa crumpled to the floor, a broken and oozing wreck of humanity.

"Dog!" cried Tehmjin. "Step from your circle and face me as a man!"

Choden sneered. However the contest looked to have weakened him. He leaned on the lectern now, breathing hard.

"Look at you," he hissed, "Hyenas circling the lion. Leave now and I'll overlook this intrusion. Stay and die. Or worse."

Sangyal glanced at Tehmjin and cursed. "What do we do? We cannot enter his circle, he cannot come out."

Choden turned to face the General, taking in his rank. "So you lead this rabble, do you?" Gathering himself up, he jabbed fingers forward in a mystic gesture. Sangyal gasped as if struck. The sorcerer, though weakened, still possessed enough will-power to freeze a man in place, to constrict muscle and twist sinew. Tehmjin cursed as spasms ran through Sangyal's now contorted form. Yisu wasted no time in cursing, she picked up a heavy flask from the table and hurled it at the scarlet-robed mage. He saw it at the last moment and dodged, the flask shattering on the wall behind. The break in concentration was enough to release Sangyal and he staggered back, gulping for air.

"Enough!" screamed the sorcerer then, thrusting arms aloft, called another word, a terrible, inhuman syllable that reverberated hard on the brains of all there. Tehmjin reeled back, the shock of that word compounded by the sight of the bodies on the slabs twitching, flopping and rising in an obscene parody of life. With unnatural speed, the reanimated corpses sprang forth to rend and tear with nails and teeth.

Tehmjin set his back to the wall, hefted his saber and snarled. The proximity of death and the presence of the supernatural stripped away any pretence of civilised behaviour. As the convulsing creature came within range, he barked and lashed out, sword a silver blur. Yet despite several wounds the corpse came on, pinning Tehmjin's arms in a steely grip, teeth snapping for his throat. The steppe-man gagged at the odour of decay and strange chemicals, twisting desperately to avoid those jaws. Letting go of his saber, he suddenly dropped down, gripping the thing's legs in both arms. He straightened and heaved, sending the corpse tumbling to the floor, then quickly scooped up his sword and chopped down hard. The blade bit into leathery flesh, cracked through brittle bone and rebounded off the flagstones. He turned the bounce into a whistling slash, sending the thing's lower jaw clattering away. Still it reached for him, until a final blow split its skull in twain, spilling forth a puddle of pale, grey ooze.

Tehmjin snatched in a lungful of air and glanced across the room. Sangyal, all finesse gone, was hewing at his attacker like a savage. The soldiers likewise fought furiously, one being dragged to the floor by two revenants. Before Tehmjin could reach them, Yisu was there, snatching up the sword of the fallen man to cut deep into the legs of both attackers. Tehmjin leapt across and between them, they hacked the pair down. Immediate danger averted, the steppe-man wheeled back to face the figure at the centre of the circle. This time, Tehmjin's eyes blazed. Blood ran in rivulets down his face, his clothing was rent in a dozen places. The slightest flicker of doubt flashed across Choden's features. It was enough. With a snarl, Tehmjin strode forward, head thrust out, dark-stained blade before him, and stepped into the circle.

Choden flung out his hands as before, conjuring that sickly violet glow, gesturing with a shout... but the glow faded. Angered, he repeated the action, with the same result. Tehmjin gave a grim laugh and pounced, slashing. The sorcerer's terror lent him speed. He gave an agile twist, dodged the strike and drew a wickedly curved knife from his robe. He cut out, but the steppe-man had already moved. Dodging past the thrust, Tehmjin stabbed his own blade forward, into Choden's chest and out between his shoulder blades. The knife fell as the sorcerer glanced down at the blade in bewilderment, clutching at it in a final act of desperation. A gout of blood erupted from Choden's mouth and his limp body slumped to the floor.

***

What remained of the troop had returned to the grove, where the guard and the escaped villagers sat waiting. Behind, a large column of smoke spiraled in the cool air as the keep burned to the ground. Sangyal, forearm bandaged, walked over to clap Tehmjin on the shoulder.

"Well, steppe-man, you earned your fee, I'll give you that."

"Someone had to kill that swine," Tehmjin grunted.

"Indeed. But why did that last spell not affect you?"

Tehmjin shrugged, then thought of the amulet Mother had given him. Perhaps there was something to all this gods business after all? He left the thought unsaid. "Just luck, I suppose. Anyway, if it's all the same, I'll take those earnings now?"

Sangyal nodded and took a pouch from his saddle pack. "It's all there, plus a little extra besides. Are you not returning with us?"

"No," the guide shook his head. "I've a mind to continue on from here to the steppe. After recent events I've a hankering for fresh air and open spaces. And Yisu can guide you back across the swamp. Besides which," he grinned as he sprang into the saddle, "that beast under the bridge might still be there. I've no inclination to fight that thing again."

The General smiled then furled his brow. "One other thing, though. What happened to the tome, the book that Jinpa was sent to retrieve?"

"Ah. Well..." Tehmjin chewed his lip. "You know you said

to set fire to the place to destroy any remnants of sorcery? Well, while you were getting patched up I cast around for something to ignite. I found a flask of fine brandy which would have burned well. But then I saw that old, papery book. No choice really." He patted the heavy flask slung off his saddle bow.

Sangyal's eyes almost popped from their sockets. "You burnt a holy book of the Order of Lheng? But... but that is sacrilege! Punishable by death!"

His face twitched in anger, his hand fell to his sword hilt. Then he paused, shoulders falling. A chuckle spasmed deep in his body. A chuckle that grew into hoots of laughter, the echoes of which followed Tehmjin as he rode back up the ridge and towards home.

ONE SWORD AGAINST THE GLUTTONOUS GODS

- Lee Clark Zumpe

Prelude

"I see no alternative." Emperor Tümen – Grand Ruler of Yothar and Defender of the Eternal Realm – gazed reverently at the arching violet blue of the cloudless heavens, quietly acknowledging their unfathomable authority and inexorable ascendancy in the lives of even the most inconsequential mortals. He felt the tug of their indomitable influence, pulling him toward an inevitable destiny. "Too many villages have already been lost, too many alliances shattered. The Mudi seers tell me his covetousness far surpasses his discretion."

"He has no army to speak of," Chimeg said. The emperor's most trusted minister, Chimeg had spent weeks trying to gauge the threat posed by Thaugnthuau, a rogue cleric turned charismatic priest. His power over the masses broadened with each passing day. "He has only his unenlightened, thick-skulled disciples, who are all ill-trained and utterly senseless."

From his palace in the capitol city of Ntha to the tallest peaks of the Borsil-uakend mountain range that served as a natural barrier between the civilized provinces of his empire and the harsh wastelands beyond, Emperor Tümen had once enjoyed the adoration of his subjects. Never in his lifetime had he faced such a grave threat, be it from a rival kingdom or from rebellious agitators plotting within his own borders. Throughout his long lifetime, his legions had never been bested in battle and he never doubted their preeminence.

Thaugnthuau – whom his disciples had designated as the Schismarch – was unlike any other rival he had encountered in 125 years on the throne.

In the face of this foe, the emperor could not help but wonder if his soldiers might finally be surpassed. He wondered if his long reign might be nearing its end, and if Yothar – proclaimed by ancient Mudi seers and the First Oracle herself as the Eternal Realm – might be as tenuous as any other failed and forgotten kingdom.

"The followers of the Schismarch may lack battlefield skill and good judgement, but they are fanatical in their devotion," the emperor said. "They would die a dozen deaths for Thaugnthuau – and with that old sorcerer's grasp of necromancy and other occult sciences, they may do just that."

i.

Sataru, personal scrivener to Emperor Tümen of Yothar, fought back ravenous shadows in the scriptorium with a self-feeding oil lamp. The clerics who once toiled night and day copying and preserving the knowledge of the ancients no longer cut their quills nor sacrificed long hours copying vital manuscripts recovered from lost civilizations that flourished before the Scathefire. Dust, dirt, and the dregs of dead languages accumulated in layers upon neglected lecterns, with inkhorns, quills, and penknives strewn across empty parchment. Only the scampering of rats in the walls kept silence from claiming dominion.

"This place smells of graves and dead men," Qadira said. With a sideways glance over her shoulder at the doorway, she found herself unable to shake the feeling that someone unseen trailed them during their long descent into the archives. The emperor insisted she accompany Sataru on his search to ensure his safety and success. The lingering stench of death seemed to validate his concern. "And I would know the reek of rotting carcasses: I've clambered through more than a few sepulchers in my time."

"You don't strike me as a graverobber, Qadira." Sataru smiled at his quip, knowing that such an insult would earn most men a sound thrashing from the chief of the Imperial Royal Guard. "But I think it is black mold and rat droppings that you find so offensive here. We are probably the first visitors to enter this chamber since access to the scriptorium was outlawed by the Conclave of Magistrates."

"Conclave of sycophants, you mean." Qadira had lost all respect for the council since the disciples of the High Priest Thaugnthuau had infiltrated it, seizing a majority of seats and desecrating its once honourable role as a reasonable and prudent advisory committee. "How many years has it been since the clerics were told not to continue their work?"

"It was almost ten years ago," Sataru said. "No one knows what became of them – not even the emperor. Once the council issued the edict, they all just disappeared."

"I was a new recruit ten years ago." Qadira smiled at an unspoken memory. "I was just another orphaned kid from a dusty border town with no future. Eshe – my mentor – saw something special in me. Without her, I'd probably be dead – or worse: I might be one of those mindless zealots that swarm like fat meat flies over the Thaugnthuau shrines."

"You are far too wise to have fallen in with those fanatics," Sataru said. "But I am glad your mentor found you. The emperor is fortunate to have such a formidable warrior and gifted military leader."

As she'd risen through the ranks of the emperor's military forces, Qadira had established herself as a skilled soldier and determined campaigner. A veteran of both the battlefield and a dozen expeditionary conquests, her exploits made her a champion among the people of Yothar. Her appointment as the chief of the Imperial Royal Guard led to celebrations across the capitol city of Ntha.

"You know far more about me about me than I know about you," Qadira said. "Although I cannot repay the compliment, I can tell you that the emperor would not waste my time and skill guarding someone he did not value very highly."

"I appreciate that," Sataru said, unable to stifle an embarrassed smile. "But I'm sure it was unnecessary. Only spiders and rodents lurk in these shadows."

"You may be correct." Qadira moved from desk to desk, allowing her lamp to shed light upon pieces of parchment that had been consigned to darkness. As she ruminated over her early years serving as a trusted member of the emperor's military forces, she paused to admire a beautifully illuminated folio from an unfinished manuscript. "But I also know that when the emperor senses peril, it's best not to ignore his concern."

"Danger or not, I prefer your company to silence and solitude." Sataru located a panel in the wall of the scriptorium precisely where Emperor Tümen indicated it would be found. Carefully, the scrivener traced its outline with his fingers, until he found an aberrant protrusion. Pressing firmly, he released the locking mechanism causing the panel to swing forward on its hinges with a prolonged, grating creak. "There it is!"

"You've found the scroll?"

"It would seem so," Sataru said, his voice awed. Despite the sincere contention of his sovereign, the scrivener had long believed the Scroll of Chuatel was no more than a figment of some sullen bard's imagination. Even the brightest scholars of the day considered it a fanciful myth – or a dangerous fabrication, depending upon which version of the fairytale they assessed. "There's no telling how long this has been hidden in this wall – no knowing how long since anyone dared to set eyes upon it."

"And now, that unpleasant task will fall upon you," Qadira said, her tone and expression exposing a sudden, genuine sympathy for her new acquaintance. "Is it true what they say? That those who read the scroll are soon beset by madness and despair?"

"If you had asked me that question yesterday, I would

have laughed," Sataru said, reluctant to employ himself in the recovery of the cursed object but equally unable to resist the temptation of its fearful possibilities. "Yesterday, I would have told you that no document has that kind of power to corrupt and pervert the mind."

"And now?"

"Now, I am no longer confident in my estimation of its significance," Sataru said, glaring nervously at the scroll he had been told to disinter. "Today, I am not sure about anything, really – except that if the fate of empire rests upon the secrets in this scroll, I have no real choice in the matter."

ii.

"I have sent a kindly, contemplative scholar on a warrior's quest." Unable to sleep, Emperor Tümen sat at a table in his private library. The chamber glowed with radiance flowing from oil lamps hung in sconces along the palace's ancient walls. A ponderous old tome with yellowed pages and an iron clasp sat before him, but its cryptic passages and colourful illuminated letters could not keep his attention. "What chance does he have at unlocking the secrets encrypted in the Scroll of Chuatel?"

"More chance than any other citizen of Yothar," Ull-naub replied. The white-haired priest wore a long red robe with flowing sleeves and a single knotted yellow belt. With eyes tightly closed, he levitated midway between the floor and ceiling while his hands moved ceaselessly, as if tracing an endless series of magical symbols in the air. "His grasp of the old languages is unparalleled. If anyone can speak that forgotten tongue, it is Sataru."

"I feel I have decreed his death." Outside, the night sky had been overrun by black clouds that shrouded the glimmering patterns of the stars. Whatever auguries they might impart would go unseen by the Mudi seers whose soothsaying guided the emperor. "For that alone, I should suffer."

"He knew what you asked of him." Ull-naub opened one eye, peering toward the sulking emperor. "Even now, he knows what may become of him. He understands that Thaugnthuau must not be allowed to stir the gluttonous gods of the Triumvirate. He is willing to make that sacrifice for you and for the people of Yothar, should it be necessary."

"This night feels far older and more measureless than one would expect." Emperor Tümen stood and walked to a nearby window overlooking the capitol city of Ntha. Parting the pale-blue velvet curtains, he gazed out over the sprawling city, its winding lanes immersed in uncanny darkness. The street lamps had been smothered. The fires in the watchtowers had been extinguished. Voracious shadows besieged every quarter. "Thaugnthuau the Schismarch walks among us, Ull-naub. What sacrifice wouldn't I be willing to make, should it be necessary?"

iii.

A noise outside the chamber suddenly drew their gazes. The low echo of hesitant footfalls and the flickering glow of torchlight bore out Qadira's uneasiness: They had not gone unseen. Among the humbler classes, it was said that the disciples of Thaugnthuau observe all things with the all-perceiving eyes of their amorphous gods of chaos, inexistence, and oblivion. Whether through divine omnipresence or by stealthy pursuit, the High Priest's underlings had managed to remain hidden until they had recovered the scroll.

"Run," Qadira said, directing her charge to flee through a door at the opposite end of the scriptorium. She placed her lamp on a nearby shelf, hoping it would not be upended in the impending fray. "Go, find another way out of here."

"I can't just leave you here – "

"I will follow you." She voiced the order in a commanding tone, reminding Sataru that as the chief of the Imperial Royal Guard, she could take care of herself. "Go!"

Like wolves mad with ravenous rage, the men of Thaugnthuau burst into the room and sprang at the warrior woman. Qadira wheeled as the first foolishly charged without taking a moment to gauge her abilities or her ferocity. She easily ducked an awkward thrust of his blade, and swiftly answered with a savage swipe that ripped a deep gash in his throat. He sank to his knees, gurgling some unintelligible entreaty to his gods before collapsing into a quivering, bleeding mass on the floor of the scriptorium.

Her attackers exhibited peculiar physical attributes: knotted muscles swelling on gaunt arms, sunken eyes that hinted at both fanaticism and insanity, blistered and diseased skin, a hideous pallidity and crusted, scabbed lips that hinted at famishment. In addition to their distinctive purple robes, they wore broken and piecemeal armour that provided little protection.

Showing more discipline than their companion, the other two disciples of Thaugnthuau hesitated as they surveyed the layout of the room and sought any elements they could use to their benefit. Less inclined to underestimate Qadira's strengths, they may have silently concluded it would be best to wait for reinforcements to arrive. They circled her anxiously, hoping time alone would be their most advantageous ally. But Qadira had already guessed their strategy. She knew that more of the High Priest's fighters would be swarming through the shadows, ready to bolster this motley group. She would not allow them the luxury of additional blades.

With a man on either side of her, she lunged to her right, turned and dipped. The foe closest to her reacted much too slowly: His blade cut through the stinking, foul air of that long-abandoned chamber without finding its mark. He grunted at his own ineptness, realizing in that moment she would not allow him a second chance. With one backward thrust, she sank her sword silently up into her adversary's lower abdomen. She felt a bloody geyser erupt as his intestines spilled out onto the floor behind her.

The final member of the original squad thanked his gluttonous gods for shielding him and granting him the glory of this victory. By far the largest and most potent of the small company, he pounced boldly, raising his sword to deliver a clean blow that would decapitate the heathen warrior who had slaughtered his companions.

Without hesitation, Qadira drew a long, slender dagger from a crimson leather sheath on her side and threw it with such precision and force that it pierced the man's gullet. The sudden pain startled her enemy, but it did not disable him. He staggered, his free hand clutching at the invading steel beneath his chin, as blood streamed over his lips. A raspy screech followed, causing frothy bubbles to ooze out of the fresh wound.

The short delay provided Qadira with ample time to finish the job. As stealthy as a jungle tiger, she moved with stunning quickness and grace. Though it took more than a single stroke to fell the brute, the chief of the Imperial Royal Guard made quick work of him. By the time he lay lifeless on the floor, Qadira had been bathed in his blood.

Before leaving the scriptorium, Qadira closed the door and fortified it by fashioning a makeshift barricade using lecterns and other heavy objects. The temporary obstacle might not be substantial enough to prohibit further pursuit, but it would impede them long enough to formalize an escape plan. Much to her surprise, Qadira found no sign of Sataru in the adjacent chamber. As her eyes grew accustomed to the darkness, she scanned the four walls of the small room but found no evidence of a doorway leading to safe passage. Yet, the absence of the scrivener offered an assurance that he had found some means of escape. She only wished he had left her a clue so that she could join him.

By now, she could hear the next wave of Thaugnthuau's bestial mercenaries trying to push their way through the impediment she had forged. Though they lacked training, dexterity, and a warrior's intuition, she perceived in them a feral malice that imbued them with cruelty, ferocity, and tenacity. Fighters like these had to be put down swiftly, because they would grapple until their last breath, taking little heed of their wounds and remaining oblivious to the likelihood of impending death.

And why would they fear death? They worshipped it. Every dying breath fed their gluttonous gods. Every untimely end satiated them. Every last gasp and every ebbing of life in their presence would be channeled to their awful, insatiable Triumvirate: chaos, inexistence, and oblivion. These gods once were worshipped under specific appellations, but even Thaugnthuau the Schismarch could not bring himself to voice their unutterable names.

For a moment, Qadira considered the fate of her own soul: Would she allow herself to become sustenance for the repugnant deities of Thaugnthuau's cult? To die alone by her own hand might spare her the injustice of that loathsome iniquity. Depriving her enemies of that minor victory would mean she died with honour, even if it meant the taking of her own life.

But, no – she could not. Qadira would stand against them for the sake of Sataru. Each one she butchered would be one less mercenary trying to pick up his trail. The chief of the Imperial Royal Guard steadied herself, took inventory of her weapons, and cycled through her best options for the forthcoming melee. She favoured the smaller of the two chambers, hoping she could slaughter the first four or five before they even barged through the narrow doorway. Their corpses would create yet another obstacle for those who followed.

When she gazed across the scriptorium, she realized that her handiwork had left her ill-prepared and witless foes scratching their heads. Their initial attempts to push through the barrier had failed, and – from the bits and pieces of their heated conversation she could discern – they disagreed over their next course of action. Pleased with her resourcefulness, Qadira withdrew back into the smaller chamber to recuperate from the recent skirmish and further prepare the next encounter, but before she could find a suitable place to rest, Qadira felt something reach up from the shadows and grasp her leg.

iv.

"This is not a contest you can win, Emperor Tümen." Chimeg arrived in the emperor's war room in time to find the Grand Ruler of Yothar donning his finest protective armour. The emperor's most trusted minister, using the most comforting tone he could muster, tried to persuade the sovereign that his personal involvement would not change the outcome of the current crisis. "You have implemented the best defence of the realm using the greatest assets at your disposal. Meeting Thaugnthuau the Schismarch face to face serves no purpose."

"How many souls will they consume?" Emperor Tümen stared at the two men trying to discourage him from action. Ull-naub, his personal priest and spiritual advisor, had summoned Chimeg when his arguments failed to sway the emperor. "How many of my citizens will die to feed their gluttonous gods? How many will fall under his spell, their eyes benighted with swirling shadows? How many sacrifices will he demand? How many will it take to usher in this new era that the Schismarch has prophesied?"

"We do not believe his prognostication is valid," Ull-naub assured him. "I confer with the Mudi seers daily, and they distrust his interpretation of the First Oracle's vision."

"Yet, everything else he has predicted has come to pass." Though nearly 150 years old, Emperor Tümen did not show his age. Extreme longevity was common in his bloodline. Several previous members of the dynasty had survived more than 300 years, watching as generations of their loyal subjects lived their lives, raised families, and died. "If we do not believe this prophecy might actually come to pass, why have we sent poor Sataru to recover the Scroll of Chuatel?"

"Because that is where hope lies," Ull-naub said. "Whatever prospect we have at restoring our good fortune is tombed and guarded by despair in some forgotten vault beneath this city. No valiant legion nor smaller brigade of hand-picked warriors could descend into the darkness and turn the tide. You know the prophecy: not ten thousand, not hundreds, not even a small squadron of a dozen fighters can be victorious. Only one single sword will bring down those demons and prevent this from becoming an empire of endless night."

That fate and future foretold by the First Oracle had sparked this unfolding catastrophe, endowing Thaugnthuau the Schismarch with the foundations of a grim crusade. His infectious fear twisted and corrupted the gullible, the simple-minded, and the misguided, making them servile pawns in his endeavour to return to an age of darkness visible. The High Priest sought to restore the ascendancy of the gluttonous gods and forebears of nature and harmony.

"In all the years you two have known me, have I ever

declined to set foot on the battlefield?" Emperor Tümen strode across the war room, scowling at his hesitance and resigning himself to his fate – whatever that may be. Between sets of banners exhibiting the colours of his many provinces, half a dozen weapons had been situated upon the wall. There they remained throughout long stretches of peace, waiting for war. "If only one sword is required, it should be mine."

As the emperor stretched to claim his sword from the wall, he heard the clang of metal and felt a sharp pain at the base of his skull. He swung around in time to see Ull-naub lying on the floor in a pool of blood ... and Chimeg – his eyes benighted with swirling shadows – raising a bloodied mace high in the air to strike a second blow.

v.

In the Dark Time that followed the cosmic destruction of the Scathefire, when all civilization was cast in ruin and most of its lingering tribes lived brief, wretched lives scattered across the wasteland, some men and women – exceptional in intellect, courage, and hopefulness – forged permanent communities. Over time, these communities blossomed into cities, city-states, and principalities. Among these shining kingdoms, none is more resplendent than Yothar, the Eternal Realm, with its glorious capitol city of Ntha. The seven golden spires of the emperor's palace can be seen from the highest peaks of the the Borsil-uakend mountain range to the low country, where fisherfolk live in quaint coastal villages along the shores of the Sea of Zstha.

Within the borders of Yothar, none are left wanting for food or shelter, none are forced into servitude, none are obligated to sacrifice more than they desire, and none fear the long-buried vestiges of the Dark Time.

\- Excerpt from the epic saga *Ultu Ulla in Ntha*

When Qadira felt cold fingers brush her ankle, she reeled back against the wall and drew her sword. Her eyes quickly found the source of the perceived peril: Sataru had unexpectedly emerged from a hidden opening in the floor.

"You nearly lost that hand, scrivener." The warrior woman scolded him with her sharp tone. She glared at him with fuming eyes a few more moments before allowing herself to smile: She was, after all, happy to see him. "I thought you had forgotten about me."

"I would not even consider it," Sataru said. "And not just because I know you would fight your way out of here, track me down, and reprimand me."

"Reprimand?" Qadira laughed. "I might do that, but only after I knocked out a few teeth." She paused, her gaze turning back to the scriptorium. The soldiers had resumed their attempts to burst through the doorway. "What have you found?"

"I am not certain, but I believe it to be a passage to the distant past. The emperor told me how to access it through a series of triggers along the wall." As he spoke, Sataru glanced downward into the pit with a disapproving grimace.

"If you thought the smell of death was strong before, you'll find it turns your stomach down here."

In the adjacent room, a loud crash and a shower of splintered wood signalled that the soldiers had made significant progress.

"They're coming," Qadira said. With the bloodlust of battle fresh in her veins, she felt the urge to stand her ground. "I can hold them off."

"For what purpose? Their deaths will only further fatten their gods," Sataru said. "Unless you just want to show off your skills with the sword some more, I think you should follow me." The scrivener abruptly plunged into the darkness. "And make sure you close the panel behind you. Thaugnthuau's mercenaries will never even find it. They will think we simply vanished."

Though unaccustomed to taking orders from a civilian, Qadira complied. As she lowered herself into the narrow pit, she found a staircase wound its way down into the eerie shadows. Sataru had explored only a fraction of its unfathomable depths, lighting torches along the moldy walls as he surveyed its secrets. His previous claim about the dank stench proved excruciatingly accurate: The mephitic reek of death pervaded the awful abyss poisoning each noxious breath of air.

"No one has walked these steps in ages," Qadira said, her keen eyes taking note of each detail as they continued their descent. Numbers and symbols had been etched upon certain stones and – at irregular intervals – long-dead workers had abandoned various implements and tools, such as picks, hammers, scrapers, and chisels. "What is this place?"

"Are you familiar with the *Ultu Ulla in Ntha*?"

"I know of it." Qadira felt a sudden rush of embarrassment. Although she could read, she had spent most of her life familiarizing herself with battlefield tactics and the biographies of great military leaders. She never found time to indulge in historical chronicles and epic sagas. "I have not read it."

"Nor have most people," Sataru said. "It's antiquated and passé, according to most modern scholars. And, unsurprisingly, the Conclave of Magistrates would prefer it remain a discarded relic, though they have not yet banned it."

"What does it have to do with this place?"

"The *Ultu Ulla in Ntha* describes the founding of Ntha and the construction of the emperor's palace." Sataru paused and put his hand on the wall. "The stones that form every barrier and floor of the capitol city came from this quarry. Our ancestors burrowed deeper and deeper beneath the surface, extracting an amazing amount of rock. Over the course of centuries, they mined stone and slate, and followed seams of precious minerals – gold, silver, and diamonds – that helped bolster the empire's treasury. Eventually, they tunnelled down so far that they reached remnants of a past civilization."

"From before the Scathefire?"

"Yes," Sataru said. "And there, according to the saga, they found palpable shadows that could not be banished by light. The author described them as 'three silhouettes with inexplicable substance, gathered together along a river of pitch.'"

"Those three shadows," Qadira said. "Those are their gods – the Triumvirate."

"And, if the *Ultu Ulla in Ntha* is to be taken as an authentic historical record, the river of pitch runs beneath each major city in the Empire of Yothar."

vi.

When Chimeg brought down the mace a second time, the emperor – though wounded – deflected the blow.

"What have you done, man?" Emperor Tümen growled at his advisor, his anger rising at the betrayal. "You have brought the wolves to our doorsteps."

"Thaugnthuau must release the gluttonous gods from their long internment." Chimeg lunged forward toward the emperor, but his scrawny body could not match his fierce intent and he stumbled as his target easily sidestepped the attack. "The High Priest will sanctify this empire of endless night and unleash the Triumvirate so they can feast upon the unworthy."

"Not if Sataru reaches the river of pitch," the emperor said. Putting distance between himself and his attacker, he hastily retrieved his sword from the wall. "Not if he uses the Scroll of Chuatel to end this seditious scheme."

"Sataru has no notion of what awaits him in the underworld." Chimeg shuffled back into a corner where a curious shadow had materialized. The traitor once again lifted the mace high in the air to make one last desperate attempt to assassinate the emperor and gain untold glory in the eyes of his new master. "Your scrivener and his protector will instead become the first offerings of flesh and bone the gluttonous gods have savoured since I led the clerics from the Scriptorium down into the caliginous depths."

Chimeg bolted from the shadow, howling a cry of rancour and madness. Emperor Tümen raised his sword and brought it down mercilessly, splitting the man's skull. Before the corpse of his former advisor could hit the floor, a second stroke severed his head from his body.

In the moment of silence that followed, the emperor appraised the situation. On the floor of his war room, the blood of two lifeless bodies pooled. His capitol city had been invaded by unnatural shadows, fervent in their desire to obliterate every source of illumination. Somewhere far beneath the neglected scriptorium, ancient gods stirred on the edges of an underground waterway that had been tainted and befouled before the Scathefire laid waste to the landscape.

One sword, the prophecy proclaimed.

He took a seat at a roundtable where his generals often gathered to plan forays or celebrate victories. He could hear voices from his past echoing through the years, extolling his accomplishments and paying tribute to the empire and its people. Those voices now felt distant and meek. Those commendations felt hollow and inconsequential. Emperor Tümen had never felt so helpless and alone.

Then, from the curious shadow in the corner, an unwanted guest appeared.

"Good evening, Emperor Tümen." Thaugnthuau the Schismarch drifted across the floor like charnel smoke in the wind. "I welcome you to my empire of endless night."

"You have no domain," the emperor said with sudden conviction. "I welcome you to your final hour, treacherous dog."

vii.

By the time Sataru and Qadira reached the end of the spiraling staircase, neither could guess how long the descent had taken nor how far underground they had journeyed. Here, darkness dwelled in perpetual dominion. It seeped from the rock and hung in the air like a feathery shroud. Their oil-fed lamps barely penetrated its tenebrous bulk as they stumbled across the rocky floor of a cavern. The blackness that permeated that chamber refused to be displaced, concealing from them its scope, proportions, and layout.

The sound of flowing water alone provided them with a destination. They scrambled forward almost blindly, depending upon the meagre glow of their lamps to keep them from falling into an unseen pit or walking into a wall.

When they reached the edge of the river of pitch, Qadira turned and looked at her companion.

"What now," she said. "What are we supposed to do?"

"The only thing I was sent here to do," Sataru replied. "Read the Scroll of Chuatel."

"But those who read the scroll are beset by madness and despair." The warrior woman clutched his arm. "There must another way."

"I may not be a soldier, but I am no different than you," Sataru said. "I am prepared to forfeit my life for the people of Yothar. Just as you risked your life for me earlier, I am prepared to make that sacrifice for you, Qadira."

Before Qadira could formulate an argument, Sataru, personal scrivener to Emperor Tümen of Yothar, sat down on the bank of the black river and, with shaking fingers, unrolled the parchment to its very end. The scroll was yellow with age, speckled with ink stains, and flecked with some gritty substance that stubbornly adhered to its surface. Around the edges, some long-dead cleric had scribbled unsophisticated illustrations that had no purposeful meaning.

At the center of the parchment, two short lines of verse had been inscribed in an ancient language.

"That's all there is?" Qadira rested her chin upon the scrivener's shoulder. "Can you even translate it?"

"Why are you looking at this?"

"It seems unlikely that something I cannot read will render me a drooling lunatic," Qadira said. "So, what does it say?"

"Nothing," Sataru said, his voice heavy with regret. "Nothing that seems useful, anyway."

"What does it say, Sataru?"

"It reads 'set alight the drowned spirit, sheath thy thirsty sword in flames.'" As Sataru ruminated over the words, he failed to notice the darkness had begun to repel the light of their oil lamps as it pressed in all around them. "Even though I can read the ancient languages, I can't untangle their meaning."

"What about the illustrations?" Qadira tapped the scroll with her finger, noticing at once the substance coating the parchment. "Is there something hidden there?"

"Nothing but insignificant doodles," he said, his tone now growing desperate and angry. "Just flames and smoke and shadow."

At that moment, the darkness sprouted a tendril that twisted itself around Qadira's leg. She hacked at it furiously with her sword, but her blade would not score it.

"I know what to do, Sataru," Qadira said, standing so that

she could face the unseen monsters striking out from the darkness. "This may sound crazy, but roll up the scroll and use the oil lamp to set it on fire."

"We're out of time, Qadira," the scrivener said, but he followed her instructions nonetheless. "I don't see what purpose this serves."

"When the scroll is burning, dip it into the river of pitch – and hurry!"

The chief of the Imperial Royal Guard continued slashing frantically at the shadows, knowing that within them lurked the gluttonous gods. She could feel their hunger as they sought to snuff out the light. Their rubbery, black limbs stretched from every conceivable angle, agile enough to ensnare her but too weak to drag her into the gloom.

"I've got it," Sataru, watching with a mix of horror and delight as flames engulfed the Scroll of Chuatel. "Just a moment – "

As he dropped the scroll into the river of pitch, the Triumvirate summoned up enough strength to pull the warrior woman into their domain. Then, the river burst into flame and banished all shadow from the vast cavern – all shadow except three silhouettes comprised of inexplicable substance, gathered together along a river of fire and light.

"The sword!" Qadira tossed her blade on the floor of the cavern at Sataru's feet. "Plunge it into the flames and withdraw it quickly!"

The scrivener again did as he was told, and when he pulled the blade from the river it seethed with fire. Sataru did not await further instruction: He charged at the gluttonous god that held his companion, striking it with the blazing sword. Its howl shook the ground and dislodged loose stones from the cavern's ceiling far above them. In agony, it relinquished its grasp on Qadira. With a knowing smile, she reclaimed her sword and began the chore of slaughtering the gods of the Triumvirate.

Afterward

In Ntha, the capitol city of Yothar, two imposing figures sat at a roundtable in the emperor's palace. Emperor Tümen – Grand Ruler of Yothar and Defender of the Eternal Realm – studied Thaugnthuau the Schismarch with troubled eyes. His distress did not stem from some lingering concern that those he entrusted to safeguard his empire and his people from an unimaginable and ghastly fate might fail. Instead, he wondered what led a man like this High Priest to rouse hatred, instigate chaos, and plunge the world into darkness and horror.

"Why?" Emperor Tümen asked of his visitor.

"Because I could," the rogue cleric turned charismatic priest replied.

No further words were exchanged between the two. When the emperor felt the time had come, he stood, walked to the only window in the chamber, and drew back the curtain. The sun's rays poured into the room, banishing the darkness.

Where Thaugnthuau had been a moment earlier, there sat only an inconsequential pile of ashes.

BIOGRAPHIES

GLYNN OWEN BARRASS

Glynn Owen Barrass lives in the North East of England and has been writing since late 2006. He has written over two hundred short stories, novellas, and role-playing game supplements, the majority of which have been published in France, Germany, Japan, Poland, the UK, and the USA.

GAVIN CHAPPELL

Over the last twenty years Gavin Chappell has been published by Penguin Books, Horrified Press, Nightmare Illustrated, Death Throes Webzine, Spook Show, and the podcast Dark Dreams, among others. He has worked variously as a lecturer, a private tutor, a tour guide, an independent film maker, and editor of Lovecraftiana: the Magazine of Eldritch Horror. His influences include Robert E Howard, Michael Moorcock, HP Lovecraft, and Terrance Dicks. He lives in northern England.

B HARLAN CRAWFORD

B. Harlan Crawford is a lapsed musician, sub-par artist, would-be writer and purveyor of the sort of low-brow schlock that is ruining this country. He festers loathsomely at his home in Tennessee with his wife, two cats and two dogs. More of his fevered scrawling can be read at https://thelibraryoftheschlocklords.blogspot.com

SHELLEY De CRUZ

Shelley wrote and illustrated her first book at the age of four. Then she had to go to school, grow up and get a proper job. Undeterred, she still manages to produce illustrations, posters and cards. There is also a stack of sketchbooks under the bed full of doodles looking for their own story. Unusually, for the female of the species, she does not like chocolate. www.facebook.com/graveheartdesigns

ASHLEY DIOSES

Ashley Dioses is a writer of dark fiction and poetry from southern California. Her debut collection of dark traditional poetry, *Diary of a Sorceress,* was released in 2017 from Hippocampus Press. Her second collection, *The Withering*, came out in 2020 from Jackanapes Press. Her poetry has appeared in *Weird Fiction Review, Cemetery Dance Publications, Weirdbook, Black Wings VI: New Tales of Lovecraftian Horror,* and others. Her poem *Cobwebs*, was mentioned in Ellen Datlow's recommended Best Horror of the Year Volume Twelve list. She has also appeared in the Horror Writers Association Poetry Showcase for her poems *Ghoul Mistress* and *Her Heart that Flames Would Not Devour* , and was a nominee for the 2019 Pushcart Prize. She is an Active member in the HWA and a member of the SFPA. She blogs at fiendlover.blogspot.com.

HR LAURENCE

H. R. Laurence grew up in North Yorkshire, and when not writing stories about swordplay he works in the film industry in London as a cameraman. His short fiction has appeared in the magazines Whetstone and Rakehell, and in the anthologies Swords and Sorceries: Tales of Heroic Fantasy; Samhain Sorceries; and Futures that Never Were. He is also the co-writer of the upcoming B-movie 'Viking Revenge'.

TIM MENDEES

Tim Mendees is a rather odd chap. He's a horror writer from Macclesfield that specialises in cosmic horror and weird fiction. A lifelong fan of classic weird tales, Tim set out to bring the pulp horror of yesteryear into the 21st Century and give it a distinctly British flavour. His work has been described as the love-child of H.P. Lovecraft and P.G. Wodehouse and is often peppered with a wry sense of humour that acts as a counterpoint to the unnerving, narratives. Tim is the author of over one hundred published short stories and novelettes, seven novellas, and two short story collections. He has also curated and edited several cosmic horror-themed anthologies. Tim is a goth DJ with a weekly radio show on The Feelgood Station, and co-presenter of the Innsmouth Book Club & Strange Shadows Podcasts. He currently lives in Brighton & Hove with his pet crab, Gerald, and an ever-increasing army of stuffed octopods. https://timmendeeswriter.wordpress.com

LYNDON PERRY

Lyndon Perry is a writer, coffee drinker, and cat herder. He lives in Puerto Rico with his wife and their 19 year old tabby, Charlie. He is also an editor and publisher of his own indie projects at Tule Fog Press. He can be found at www.lyndonperrywriter.com

ROBERT POYTON

Robert is the founder of *Innsmouth Gold*, set up as an outlet for his music and literary projects. A long-time fan of weird fiction and Sword and Sorcery, Robert is a professional musician, writing and performing with garage-horror band *The Phobias*. He is also an experienced martial arts instructor, having published a wide range of books and films on Chinese and Russian arts. Born and raised in East London, Robert now lives in rural Bedfordshire, where he enjoys making a noise and swinging sharp objects around.

RUSSELL SMEATON

Born from an egg on a mountain top, Russell has spent the past 40-something years doing stuff and things. After spending a decade travelling around the world he has now settled down in the North of England. He lives with his lovely family and a few errant cats, who know far more than they should. Luckily they're not telling.

LEE CLARK ZUMPE

Lee Clark Zumpe has been writing and publishing horror, dark fantasy and speculative fiction since the late 1990s. His short stories and poetry have appeared in *Weird Tales, Space and Time* and *Dark Wisdom*; and in anthologies such as *The Children of Gla'aki, Best New Zombie Tales Vol. 3, Through a Mythos Darkly, Heroes of Red Hook* and *World War Cthulhu*. His work has earned several honourable mentions in *The Year's Best Fantasy and Horror* collections.

As entertainment editor for Tampa Bay Newspapers, his work has been recognized repeatedly by the Florida Press Association, including a first place award for criticism in the 2013 Better Weekly Newspaper Contest. Lee lives on the west coast of Florida with his wife and daughter. Visit www.leeclarkzumpe.com.

ACKNOWLEDGEMENTS

We would like to give thanks to everyone who helped
make this book possible.

To our authors and artist for sharing their talents.

To all those who backed the project and
helped spread the word, including:
Chris Karr, Ricky Broome, Deborah Dubas Groom, Riju Ganguly,
Harry Baker, John A DeLaughter, Red Duke Games, Tony Bradbury,
Apollo Lammers, Richard Paladino, Schlock Webzine,
Happy Steitz, Robert Avritt, Christopher Lackey, Hampire Ham,
Anthony Deming, Chris Kalley, Balki, Barbaric Splendor,
Francisco Vera, L.E.D., Peter Aldin, FredH, Miguel Fliguer,
David Malaski, Jill Vance, Chris Jarocha-Ernst, Stewie, and
the Innsmouth Writing Circle.

If you have enjoyed this book, please
post a review on Amazon. Thanks!

www.innsmouthgold.com

For the latest info on new releases, special offers and events,
sign up to our *Innsmouth Whispers* newsletter.
You'll get a 20% discount voucher on joining!

http://eepurl.com/hysilb

ANCESTORS AND DESCENDANTS

This anthology explores prequels and sequels to Lovecraftian tales. You will discover the dark history of the de la Poers, read of the early days of the artist Pickman, and learn the secrets of Erich Zann.

From downtown Arkham to distant Venus, this unique illustrated collection expands and explores the rich legacy left to us by the Father of the Weird Tale.

WEIRD TAILS

Lovecraft loved cats! So we gathered together new weird stories with a distinctly feline theme!

From unearthly Ultharians to the humble house moggy, from temple guardians to witch's familiar, you might never look at your cat in the same light again...

Portraits of Terror

The Innsmouth Writing Circle brings you new tales of the weird and the Lovecraftian, all based on the theme of the Arts.

From doomed musicians, to magical paintings, from lost Shakespeare plays to unworldly sculptures. Thirteen tales that may well change your perspective on Art and Creation...

CORRIDORS

Something happened. The world changed.
Now, we live underground in labyrinthine
complexes, our lives overseen by the Ministry.
For only they have access to our Ruler...
The King in Yellow.

13 tales in a new setting based on the King in Yellow mythos of Robert W Chambers.

THE DUNWICH TRILOGY

Milton Keynes UK
Ingram Content Group UK Ltd.
UKHW011908090224
437550UK00011B/362